Adoring the Architect

Cowboys & Angels Book 26
George H. McVey

Introduction

Aileen McRae took one look at the handsome man at her brother's wedding and knows he is the man for her. Only one problem: her brother forbids the man from even talking to her. What's a woman supposed to do to get courted by the man of her dreams? Break the rules, of course.

Sterling McCormick is the most unlucky man in the game of love in all of Creede. Every woman he tries to court falls in love and marries- someone else. So when he sees the most lovely red-haired, gray-eyed woman at Edwin McRae and Millie's wedding, he knows she is meant for him. If only Edwin would stop acting like an ogre and allow them to court.

Can love overcome an over protective brother? Can Sterling make it through one picnic without losing the woman's affections? How about Aileen? Will she finally become the bride after all these years of watching over her family? In Creede, anything is possible with a little angelic help. After all, someone has to be Adoring the Architect, don't they?

Dedication

This one is for all the readers who waited so patiently for it. Enjoy.

Table of Contents

Prologue

Sterling McCormick stepped into Pastor Bing's church in Bachelor to watch yet another lady he'd been interested in courting get married. That Millie Bing had chosen Edwin McRae over him hadn't been a surprise. He'd badly handled the incident with the angry men trying to stop her March for Women's Right to Vote. Sterling had honestly been worried about her and how violent those men seemed. He'd reacted out of fear, and McRae won the day with his bullheaded support of Millie's March and cookie giveaway. Now here he was again, watching a woman he'd tried to court marry another. *That's the last time I try to court a woman with a picnic. I just seem to have the worst luck with picnics and love.*

He looked around, trying to find an inconspicuous place to support his friend. While he didn't like losing a woman as good and sweet as Millie, she was still his friend and McRae was still a fine upstanding man. However, he also knew the stubborn Scot could hold a grudge. So he wanted to show them there weren't any hard feelings on his end of things, but he didn't want to be in their face about it either. It seemed, however, that his luck was holding steady and the only open seat he could see was right down front on the right side of the church, directly in sight line of the bride and groom. With a slight nod to Edwin, he made his way to the pew beside Hugh Fontaine. Not long after he took his seat, the doors opened and in came a younger woman with dark hair and blue eyes. She walked to the front to stand at the altar. Who was this young woman who stood with Millie? She was followed in by another young woman similar enough in appearance to be her sister; she too walked to stand at the altar.

Everyone stood as Reverend Bing slipped out the door to escort his sister into the church. It startled Sterling as another woman, older than the first two, entered. She was beautiful, with her fiery red hair, and skin so porcelain smooth and creamy that her beauty overwhelmed him. Like the two women before her, she strode to the altar, but unlike the others she moved with a bearing so regal that she might well have been a queen. She took her place at the altar and turned, facing the congregation. Her eyes met his, and Sterling felt his heartbeat quicken in his chest. His eyes were locked on hers, and he felt himself getting lost in the deep pools of bluish gray that held his attention. As he gazed into her eyes, he wondered why he'd ever wanted to court any other woman. Everyone he knew were pale imitations of the perfect specimen of womanhood before him now. He would find out who she was, and he would court her. Nothing or no-one was going to keep this woman, this regal and perfect lady from being his wife. She was his and his alone; she just didn't know it yet.

He was startled from his thoughts as Hugh slapped him on the back and tugged on his coat. He noticed everyone around him was seated, and he quickly sank down beside his friend. Reverend Bing said something to Edwin that caused the man to frown, but it all was lost on him as his eyes connected with the beauty standing just to Millie's right. She seemed to be as connected to him as he was to her, and he knew the day wouldn't be complete until he found out who she was and where she was staying. If he'd learned anything in the past few encounters, it was to strike first and fast when it came to winning a lady's affection, and he wouldn't lose this lady. No, this one was his.

Aileen was exhausted, not just from the journey, though the three weeks felt much longer with the constant motion first of the ship and now of the train. No, she was weary all the way to her soul. She'd never been more grateful than when the Vicar handed her the short wire from Edwin just over a month ago. Thanks to her and her refusal to allow the current Laird of the Aberdeen Locality to take her as his mistress, he'd first had her and her sisters put out of the cottage they'd lived in their whole lives stating that the cottage was needed for the new groundskeeper. Subsequently, as soon as his mother had passed, whom Aileen was a paid companion for, she was terminated and not given the position of Nanny his mother had promised her, as had his wife.

Afterwards, using the influence of his position, he'd had both Isla and Rhona removed from their jobs as well. Of course, both employers had said it was the settlement's failing economy, but later the Vicar had admitted that he'd been ordered to release Rhona or be replaced himself. He'd done what he could though and allowed the three of them to stay in his stable loft until word of that had gotten back to the Laird as well. Thankfully, that was the day Edwin's wire and funds had arrived. She'd wasted no time getting her sisters to the port and bought passage for them to New York, then sent a quick wire back to Edwin. Now here they were, about to start their new life in America and what better way to do so than to watch Edwin marry Millie Bing.

Aileen hugged her new sister-in-law one last time as her sisters walked down the aisle of Reverend Bing's church, and then she entered herself. Though it had been almost a year since her Da had passed away, she remembered how he'd always told her to keep her head high because the blood of old highland kings flowed in her veins. She smiled just a little and did as he'd taught her, moving slowly, and she hoped regally, with her head held high all the way to the front where she took her place beside her sisters. She heard her brother's intake of breath and looked up to see Millie enter the church, but her eyes were caught and her own breath faltered at the sight of the tall, dark-haired, handsome man sitting in the second row. It was like a thread of belonging connected her to him, and she couldn't tear her eyes away even for a second. Who was this man? His eyes were deep and dark, and she felt their pull all the way in her very spirit.

She startled back into the present when her sister Isla tugged on her arm. "Come on, Aileen. We're catching a ride back to the Hearth and Home with Edwin's partners, the Fontaine's. What's wrong with ya, anyway? Ya been standing there staring at that same spot since you walked up here."

Aileen felt the blush that was climbing up her neck, and she half smiled at her sister. "Just tired, I suppose. You said we were riding back to Creede with Winnywin's partners?"

"Aye, Edwin has made arrangements for us to take rooms at the boarding house. In return, we'll help out both the Fontaine's with the boarding house and Edwin with the restaurant. Ye must be very tired. Edwin told us all this on the way up here to the church."

Aileen didn't answer, lost again in her thoughts of the handsome gentleman whom she'd seen, wondering who he was and how to get him to come calling. A gentle warmth filled her, and she could almost hear her Da's voice in her ear. "Slow down, me bonnie lass. Ye'll ken the man soon enough."

She nodded and climbed into the back of the buggy with the help of Hugh Fontaine. Soon enough, after all, if he was interested he knew where she'd be. Didn't he?

One

Sterling woke the next morning and quickly dressed. He hoped that at church this morning he would see the woman who had caught his attention. He knew she must be one of Edwin's sisters whom everyone had said arrived just a few hours before the wedding from Scotland. Sterling wondered which church Edwin would choose to attend this Sunday. He knew the man had attended Reverend Theodore's church until he'd taken an interest in Millie and then, like Sterling, he'd started making the trip up the mountain to the church in Bachelor, mostly to spend time with Millie.

While Sterling had also been going to spend time with Miss Bing now Mrs. McRae, he'd keep going because it gave him a chance to do some woodworking that didn't involve building business or homes. He enjoyed the carving and detailed work that the local men put on the pulpits and communion tables they built to help support the church in Bachelor. Not only that, but the sermons were more uplifting and encouraging. He always felt like he'd been found lacking when he sat through Eugene Theodore's sermons. However, today while he knew he should be focused on the sermon and worship, all he wanted was to find out the name of the woman who'd haunted his dreams and consumed his waking moments.

Finally, he climbed aboard his horse and headed up the mountain. He arrived and noted that Callum Bing seemed a bit more flustered than normal. His suit was not well pressed and his tie was slightly crooked. It made Sterling smile to realize that the normally so seemingly perfect minister was having trouble without his own sister to see to his domestic needs. He laughed when the McRae's entered, and Millie went straight to Callum and straightened his tie and shook her head at the condition of his suit. His laughter died, however, when the red-haired beauty from the day before entered the sanctuary. He stood and walked toward her when Edwin suddenly appeared between him and the lady he wished to get to know. "Stop right there, McCormick. Ye'll not be trying yer courtship game on me, sisters. Ye'll be staying away from Aileen, or I'll be seeing you out back. You ken what I'm telling ya?"

Sterling was shocked. "Edwin, I don't understand. Why are you so upset with me? What have I ever done that's made you not even want to introduce me to your family? I thought we were friends."

Edwin crossed his arms over his chest. "You aren't my friend. You're a neighbor, but you also have a terrible reputation for trying to woo every eligible woman around. My sisters are here to help me with the restaurant and find decent husbands, not a rake like you."

Sterling shook his head. "Why would you call me a rake? I've not taken advantage of any woman in my life."

"Oh, no? Let's see, how many women have you courted since you arrived here after the fire? There was Mariah Redding, who became Mrs. Jensen, but not until after you courted her, then who was next? Oh yes, Nessa Dobbs, who left here and returned to New York after being courted by you. Next you tried to court Regina Stoker, not to mention all the Crowther sisters and finally, my own Millie. Why I even heard that you were seen in the Nugget consorting with the woman there, Celeste. So I call you a rake, a womanizer with no intent to marry any of them."

Sterling's face heated up as his Irish temper got away from him. "That's not even remotely true. I went on one outing with Miss Redding, who told me she was attracted to her now husband. Nessa was not a courtship, she and I provided chaperones for her sister and Aedan during their courtship. I never tried to court Regina. I helped her out when she arrived in town, as did several others. How can you or anyone say I was ever interested in any of the Crowther girls? Those girls are relentless in chasing men in this town. Even Reverend Theodore was forced to marry one of them. As for your own wife, she made it plain that she preferred you over me, and I instantly stepped aside. As for that woman in the saloon, I did nothing with her and whoever told you otherwise is a liar."

He looked over Edwin's shoulder at his sister. "Yes, I've courted a couple of women. Why shouldn't I? Don't I deserve a wife and family?" He shifted his gaze to Edwin. "Are you the only one allowed to find a wife?"

Edwin puffed himself up and pointed a finger at Sterling. "I don't care if you find a wife. I only care that it won't be one of my sisters. LEAVE THEM ALONE!"

Reverend Bing hurried to them as Edwin's yelling drew attention. "Gentlemen, you are both in the Lord's house. This is unacceptable."

Sterling looked at the Reverend and nodded. "I apologize, Reverend Bing. I'll leave so that there is no other disturbance to your services."

He shoved past Edwin and smiled at Aileen as he passed her. She gazed up at him and smiled shyly back. Sterling continued outside and climbed on his horse. He'd head to his house and spend the morning working on the rebuild. He needed to pound something, and since it would be wrong to pound on Edwin McRae in the house of God, he'd go pound some nails instead. Even so, he looked back at the church once as he rode away thinking. He would find a way to court Aileen McRae no matter what her bull-headed brother said. She was going to be his wife, even if it took everything he had to accomplish it.

The morning after her brother was married, Aileen was startled awake by someone calling her name in her room at the hearth and home. As she sat up, she almost screamed out loud as she saw her Da standing at the foot of her bed. It wouldn't have been such a shock if he hadn't been dead and buried right before everything went wrong back in Crawton. "Da?"

Her Da smiled at her and nodded his head. "It's truly me, my bonnie lass."

Aileen shook her head "Cain't be; you're dead and buried. I must be dreaming or going daft."

"Nay, lass yer as awake as can be. Your Mam and me, we got assigned ta look after you lot. 'Course yer Mam she had ta be first. Took care of ya brother and his wife, she did. Wanted ta be the one ta look after ya as well, but I put me foot down. Ye have been me bonnie lass since the day ye came into the world. I tole her ta leave ya be and let me handle things. So here I be and we got lots ta do."

Aileen cocked her head to the left slightly as she pondered the words her Da was saying. "I don't ken what ya are saying Da. What do ya mean you got assigned ta look after us?"

"I mean HISSELF done gave us the assignment ta guard you and yer brother and sisters. We're ta make sure ya all are safe and guide ya and the ones meant fer ya together. Once ye be settled and cared for, then we'll be moving on ta other assignments."

She shook her head. None of this made sense to her, so she reached down and pinched herself, yelping when it hurt. Her Da looked upset. "I done tole ya this isn't a dream. I'm really here, lass. Tis your Angel I am, and you need to get up and get dressed. Today ye will get introduced to the man who caught your eye yesterday."

Aileen watched her father slowly faded until she couldn't see him. She thought about his words and the fact that her Da was her Angel. She wondered what that meant? Not only that, but she wondered at him saying Mam had something to do with Edwin and Millie's marrying. As she pondered on the things she'd been told, she got up and dressed in the new dress Edwin had bought her before his wedding.

He had told the woman at the mercantile that she, Isla, and Rhona would all be back on Monday to get more clothes and anything else they needed. Everything was to be put on his account, which he told his sisters was the way it was done in Creede. That women didn't pay in cash at either Crowther's Dry Good's or the mercantile because it wasn't safe for women to have money on their person. She wondered about that and had planned to talk to some other women and see if that was true.

Aileen and her two sisters rode to church with Edwin and his new wife. The two had shown up at breakfast, and Aileen could tell that Millie was exactly what her brother needed. As the oldest, she had helped to raise each of her siblings and knew that she felt more like the Nanny and second mam at times instead of their sister. Yet she loved each of them and hoped that this fresh start would lead them to a love like it appeared Edwin had found.

When they pulled up to the church that Edwin's brother-in-law pastored, Aileen felt like there was a mass of fluttery creatures swarming in her belly. Her Da indicated this morning that she'd get a right proper chance at meeting that handsome lad from the wedding. The only place she thought that might happen was at the church. Millie explained to them that services here consisted of the worship service followed by a sort of bible class with the women and children inside and the men outside.

The women worked on making a quilt that was to be sold in Denver to help support the church, since the people of the church were mostly poor. A potluck dinner would follow that on the grounds. "We won't be able to have the potluck much longer as the weather will turn cold and snow will fall. There was some talk about moving the potluck indoors into the old Saloon that Edwin's partner Hugh Fontaine used to own but nothing has been decided yet."

Just then they walked inside, and Millie muttered under her breath. "Ach! Callum not even gone a day and ye can't get yourself together."

She made a quick walk to the preacher and fussed over him. Just then Aileen's attention was drawn to the man who stood and started walking straight to her. His eyes locked on her just as hers locked on him. He was but a few steps away when Edwin suddenly moved in front of her, blocking the man from reaching her. "Stop right there, McCormick," her brother fairly roared. "Ye'll not be trying yer courtship game on me, sisters."

From beside her, she heard her Da groan. "What is that dunderhead eejit doing? The lad's a right fine man, and Edwin should be happy he wants to be introduced to you."

Nevertheless, Edwin wasn't happy. He went on and soon the two men were arguing, their voices growing louder. Edwin accused him of courting several of the women in town and never proposing to any of them. Her Da grew more irritated with every name Edwin threw out. "Half that ain't even true. That brother of yours appears ta be jealous of the man still. Just because he had set his fancy on Millie, and she took her time to decide which man she wanted, is no reason to keep you from finding happiness."

Aileen startled at her Da's announcement and whispered to him. "Ye mean he courted Millie at the same time Edwin was?"

The angel nodded. "Aye, lass. But they both realized quickly that they weren't right for each other."

As she was listening to her Da, it looked like Edwin and Mr. McCormick were about to come to blows. Then the preacher stepped between them and spoke "Gentlemen, you are in the Lord's House; this is unacceptable."

Mr. McCormick nodded to Reverend Bing. "I apologize Reverend, I'll be leaving so there is no further disturbance to your services."

He pushed past Edwin and slowed for a moment as he drew close to Aileen and smiled at her, setting her pulse to racing. She shyly smiled back at him, hoping her brother didn't pick up on it. Thankfully, she could watch him walk out the door without upsetting Edwin as almost every person in the church watched as the man she now knew was named Sterling McCormick stomped away.

Before she could say a word to Edwin about how rude he had been, his new wife was there doing it for her. She couldn't help but grin as Edwin took the quiet dressing down that his new bride gave him all the way to the front of the church where she sat them all.

Throughout services Aileen wondered how she could meet the man officially and if he would listen to her eejit of a brother and stay away. She tensed at the thought. Aileen was almost thirty-five and didn't have many more chances at a marriage at all, and Sterling McCormick took her breath away. She determined right then that she would find a way to meet the handsome builder and pray his interest in her continued; despite Edwin and his boorish behavior.

Two

Sterling woke sore from all the work he had done the day before. He'd gotten a lot of the front second story framed and some of the siding up as well. He pounded nails and manhandled wall boards that should have taken two men all by himself, all the time burning with anger over the way Edwin McRae had treated him. When he'd finally fallen into bed back at his rental shack, he'd been asleep dreaming of red hair and bluish-gray eyes almost before his head hit the pillow.

Climbing out of bed, he washed his face and dressed for the day. Normally, he'd cook himself some eggs and bacon, but today he realized he was out of both. He'd need to make a trip to the mercantile before he could cook for himself. Since he had to go to a restaurant for breakfast anyway, and he was still so upset with Edwin, he thought he'd go to the Hearth and Home just to make the man cook for him. As an added bonus maybe he'd be able to see Aileen for a few seconds, even get to talk to her. He knew from listening to others talk after the wedding that Edwin's sisters came to help him with the restaurant. Hopefully, Aileen would be a server, not a cook.

He grabbed his hat and headed to the Hearth and Home, when a man who was dressed in a kilt that looked an awful lot like the tartan that Edwin had worn at the Votes for Women March, walked up beside him. "Well lad, ye should be asking her iffen ye can court her after ye meet her today."

Sterling frowned, the man had a serious Scottish brogue that was so thick it was hard to understand. "I'm sorry, are you talking to me?"

The older man nodded. "Aye, who else would I be talking to? Are ye daft or something?"

"No, I'm not daft. However, I am confused; who are you and what are you talking about?"

The Scot laughed. "Who I am isn't consequential, it's Aileen that's significant. You should ask her to allow ya to court her."

"I haven't even been introduced to her."

"Well, I expect ye'll be getting an introduction at breakfast, lad. Pay attention now and don't be putting your courtship on its beams end afore ye get off the starting line."

"Who are you and how do you know who I'm interested in?" Sterling asked as he looked over at the man who was suddenly not beside him. He stopped and looked all around. The stranger was just gone, there was no sign of him anywhere. He shook his head and started walking to the boarding house and restaurant.

Sterling opened the door to the Hearth and Home, the smiling face of the very woman he was hoping to see greeted him. "Good morning, Mr. McCormick. Are you here for breakfast?"

He smiled back at her, pulling his hat off his head as he did so. "Good morning to you, Miss McRae. Yes, breakfast would be delightful, though your lovely smile has almost made me forget my hunger this morning."

As if to call him a liar his stomach grumbled loudly causing the delightful woman to giggle like a schoolgirl. "I think your stomach has something to say about that blarney your mouth is spouting."

He grinned and shrugged his shoulders. "I said almost, Miss McRae."

"Aye, that ye did."

She led him to a table along the inside aisle where he wasn't visible from the kitchen when the door should open. He looked into her gray eyes, causing her to blush a bit. "Are you trying to keep your brother from seeing me here, Aileen?"

She gasped at his use of her first name, and he grinned even bigger. "We may as well use each other's given names, lass, as I plan on courting and making you my wife."

Her hand flew to her chest. "Sterling, you presume too much. We haven't even been introduced and if my brother has his say we never will."

He turned to her and took her other hand in his. "Then let's make sure he doesn't get his say. Allow me to introduce myself. I'm Sterling McCormick, the local architect and builder. I'm also the man who is asking to court you and eventually marry you."

She leaned close to him. "I am not opposed, but my brother seems to be. We should meet somewhere away from here and the prying eyes and ears of my family."

"I am not opposed to that, yet it will need to be someplace where your reputation will be safe. Are you serving all day?"

She smiled at him. "Today I am, well except I have a trip to the mercantile planned for between breakfast and lunch."

"I need to go to the mercantile around that same time. Perhaps we can meet there and make a plan for a courtship while we shop."

She bit her bottom lip, causing Sterling to want to kiss her so badly. Yet he knew if he attempted, somehow Edwin would find out, and it would stop their plans before they even got started. The bell on the front door rang as Reverend Bing stepped in, looking frazzled. "I shall meet you there." Aileen whispered before she went to welcome the Reverend. Sterling settled into the seat and waited as her younger sister came to take his order. He smiled and ordered, then ate quickly and left, determined to check on his builders at the various projects they were working on around town before meeting Aileen at the mercantile.

Aileen watched as Sterling finished his breakfast and then left with a nod of his head and a secret smile just for her. Her heart raced thinking about meeting him later that morning at the mercantile and planning how to court in secret. She turned her mind to that as she worked for her sister-in-law, who had taken her husband and went with the Reverend Bing to do something in the town of Topaz. Millie had come back from meeting with her brother during the breakfast rush and asked Edwin to come with her to Topaz and then asked Aileen and her sisters to keep the kitchen running until they returned. Aileen had promised them that they would and when the breakfast rush was over, and the dishes cleaned she turned to Rhona and Isla

"Will the two of you finish preparing the lunches for the miners and workers? I need to run to the mercantile really quick and order some things. When I return one of you can go and pick up more clothes and necessities, and we will each take turns today so two of us are here at the restaurant at all times until Millie and Edwin get back."

Isla looked at her and smiled. "Would your going first have anything to do with a certain gentleman who came to see you during breakfast?"

Aileen knew she was blushing. "I don't know who you are referring to, and even if I did, nothing could come of it. You saw how Edwin was yesterday. I don't know who he thinks he is dictating who I can court or not. Anyway, I will not allow my personal life to become fodder for your gossip, sister."

She looked pointedly at Isla, who just laughed. "Get on with ya then. But I'd be careful or ye will be testing that determination about Edwin sooner rather than later."

She nodded, knowing that Isla spoke the truth. As much as she was determined to make her own way here in this new land, her little brother would be a typical highlander man thinking he had some say in her future. She, however, had led this family since their Mam died, and she refused to let Edwin think he had any say in who she courted or married; if an old maid of thirty-five could marry.

That thought still rattling around in her brain, she grabbed her reticule and placed her bonnet on as she headed for the mercantile. She crossed the street and was greeted by the very man she knew she would see at the store. Sterling surprised her by asking, "Miss McRae, would you do me the honor of having a cup of tea at the tea shop with me before I escort you to the mercantile?"

"Aye, a spot of tea sounds lovely, Mister McCormick; I didn't know that Creede had a tea shop."

"It does. Two sisters from England opened it just a few months ago. The tea there is very good and the scones and biscuits, as they call them, are divine."

They took a turn away from Main Street, and Aileen took Sterling's arm. The handsome builder smiled at her before giving her a word of warning. "I know you were just planning on going to the mercantile, but please be careful. There are some immoral men in Creede and as much as Marshal KC and his deputies try to keep everyone safe, women are still being snatched right off the street. Make sure you go nowhere alone."

She was a bit put out at his attitude, but before she let her temper get the best of her; she took a moment and realized he was trying to keep her safe. "I've been on me own for quite some time, Mister McCormick, I can take care of myself if need be."

He opened the door to the tea shop for her and leaned close as she entered. "Of that I have no doubt, Aileen. However, I want you safe and cared for. If not for Edwin being an idiot about me, I would escort you personally any, and everywhere you wished to go."

His comment caused a warm delicious feeling to settle in her core as she knew he meant every word. "My brother is an eejit and has no real say over who I see or court or whom I walk out with. I am a woman; full-grown and able to speak my own mind."

"Yes, you are, but it was you who wanted to meet and discuss courting away from your brother's eyes and ears."

She nodded, "That I did, but more for your sake than mine, Sterling McCormick. My brother has a bit of a temper, as you saw yesterday. What I don't understand is that from everything I've heard, you and he got along fine until he started courting Millie. No one understands his anger over you trying to get an introduction to me. Millie and a few others said he acts as if he's jealous of you."

Sterling smiled at her. "Did they now? Well, I honestly don't know why he reacted the way he did yesterday. Millie made it very plain to me who she wanted, and I stepped aside the moment she clarified she was in love with Edwin. I hold them no ill will and pray they have a happy life together and are blessed with many offspring."

She smiled at Regina Honeycutt as she came up to them. "Aileen, it's good to see you again. I see that despite your brother's attempt to keep you and Mr. McCormick apart yesterday, you found each other anyway."

Aileen blushed as Sterling laughed. "How is it you know already about Edwin's little tantrum, Regina?"

The Englishwoman smiled. "You'll learn quickly here in Creede that even though the town is growing, gossip makes the rounds faster than a windstorm. Why, all the ladies knew by supper time last night how Mr. McRae and Mr. McCormick almost came to blows over you in Bachelor's church. I also know that Mr. McCormick spent the day taking his frustrations out on his house instead of your brother. Now what can I get the two of you?"

Sterling smiled up at the woman. "A pot of your Earl Grey and a plate of those wonderful lemon blueberry scones your sister makes, if you have them, Mrs. Honeycutt."

"A perfect choice for courtship, Mr. McCormick. I'll be right back with them."

Aileen blushed. "Keeping our plans quiet seems like it's going to be quite the feat in Creede."

Sterling nodded. "I imagine eventually your brother will get wind of it. Does that bother you?"

She thought for a moment before answering. "Only in that I don't like to see him upset. He needs to realize that while he was here making his fortune, I was back home running our family. I will not let anyone, including him, tell me whom I may or may not court or even marry. That decision is mine and mine alone to make. You've not shown me any reason to turn your suit away, and we both know there is something here so I will allow you to court me.

Just not where it will cause a fight every time you come to call on me."

"I will agree to that for now, but I won't pretend not to be courting you if he asks me, Aileen. I'm not ashamed of who I am, nor will I hide from your brother as if courting you is wrong."

Just then Regina came over with the teapot and scones on a try. "Oh, courting in secret; how very romantic. Why, it's like those stories my sister is always reading. Star-crossed lovers and secret rendezvous."

She winked at Aileen. "Don't worry, I'll keep your secret but know that eventually the word will get out, and your brother will know about you two."

Aileen nodded. "Aye, I'll deal with that when it happens."

The shop owner nodded and left them to their tea. They talked and got to know each other and sooner than she wanted it was time to hurry to the mercantile and get her dresses and things so that she could get back and help her sisters prepare for the supper crowd. As they parted ways, Sterling asked if he could see her again on Wednesday. "Aye, maybe we can go for a late picnic."

His face went white. "How about I take you to the hotel restaurant for a late dinner or early supper? Picnics and I don't work out very well."

She nodded and was shocked when he pulled her to the side of the Hearth and Home out of sight of the main boardwalk. "May I kiss you, Aileen, before we part?"

Her heart raced as she looked at his lips. "Aye, Sterling McCormick, I wish you would."

Then her world exploded in heat and color, as his lips captured hers, drinking their fill. When he released her, she swayed for a moment, not remembering where she was or even knowing if her legs would hold her up. Then she straightened herself and rubbed his cheek with her hand. "That was lovely."

He smiled "Yes it was. I hope to get more wonderful kisses on Wednesday then, my dear."

She smiled at him as she walked back around.

"We shall see, lad, we shall see." She hurried inside the restaurant and got back to work, all the while feeling his lips against hers in her memory.

Three

Aileen was tired after supper service and took herself to the small room in the attic of the boarding house she had claimed as her own. Both Millie and Julianne had tried to talk her into taking a room on the second floor like her sisters, but Aileen knew they meant guests to use those rooms. She was perfectly happy in one of the small worker's rooms up in the attic. In reality, her sisters should have taken two of them as well, but she was sure that her younger, pretty sisters would soon have men come calling, men looking for a wife. Men her brother wouldn't have a single problem allowing them to court.

No, only the man she was interested in, the man who was fascinated by her, would be the one her brother would refuse to even consider as a match for any of them. She still couldn't get the feel of that kiss off her lips. Her sisters had pestered her all day for the reason for her dreamy expression after she came home from shopping, so she knew they realized something more than shopping had taken place. She just prayed that they'd not say anything to Edwin or there would be a battle.

Sterling was the man for her. She knew it, and her Da had all but confirmed it by showing up and telling her what a good and fine man he was. She was going to let him court her, kiss her, and when he asked she was going to marry him, even if her brother didn't approve.

Just as she was preparing to change into her nightgown, there came a knock at her door. She sighed and walked over to open it to Edwin's smiling face. "I have good news for ye, lass."

"What are you yammering about, Winnywin? I thought you were out with Millie helping Reverend Bing meet up with his wife-to-be."

Her brother smiled. "Aye, I was, and that's where your good fortune comes in. After we rode to Topaz and the lass agreed to marry Callum, we followed them over to South Fork for their wedding, and after that I ran into an old friend of mine, Angus MacGregor. He owns a spread over in South Fork. I didn't know he'd settled here. He and I came over on the boat from the old country. He's a fine Scottish highlander, lass, and he's looking ta find him a good Scottish lass for a wife. I told him all about ye, and he's downstairs waiting ta meet ya."

Fear shot through her at Edwin's words, followed by anger. "Ye brought him here with ye, brother? Without talking to me first to see if I was even interested in meeting the fella?"

Edwin's face showed his confusion. "I just thought of you when he mentioned looking for a Scottish lass to wed. He's a bit too old for either Rhona or Isla, lass. Nevertheless, he's just forty years old and would be perfect for ya. Now come downstairs and meet the lad, for crying out loud."

"No! I'll not be going to meet yer mate lad, not tonight, not ever. Who do ye think ye are, telling me who I can court, or can't court? According to yer neighbors, a perfectly good man wanted to be introduced to me yesterday, and ye ran him off without a how do ya do. Today ye bring a man you just reconnected with from a boat ride ye had years before and tell me he'll make me a fine husband. Tell me, Edwin McRae, what do you know of this Angus MacGregor since he got off that boat all them years ago? How do you know he's a good man? Hmm?"

She could see Edwin's anger building behind his eyes. He was shocked too; he'd never known her to refuse anything their Da had told her to do, and he thought he had the right to demand the same compliance from her. Well, he had another think coming to him. She was his sister, his older sister at that, she'd helped change his nappy and watched over him as a babe. He wasn't about to step into their Da's shoes now. Especially since he left home years ago without a thought to what would happen to her or their sisters when Da passed away.

"Ye will come down and meet him, Aileen. It's only proper. He came all this way to meet with you. He is a perfectly fine man, and a Scotsman at that. I won't be putting up with your sass tonight, lass. Now come along."

She placed her hands on her hips and glared at him. "Nay laddie, I'll not be going anywhere tonight nor will I meet this man any other time. Ye have no say in who I court or even who I wish to be introduced to. If I remember right yer own wife marched with you alongside her so that we women had the right to our own say in our lives. So you tell yer bloody Scotsman that he made the trip fer nothing. I'll not be part of yer little scheme. I'll be choosing me own beau and giving me own permission for courting me. Not you, laddie. Not now, not ever, and even ye don't like my choice, then ye'll be keeping that ta yourself or we will be having words. Do ye ken what I'm saying to ye?"

Her brother stood nose to nose with her. "I done told the lad he had my permission ta court ya. Now come down and meet the man, or I'll haul you down there over my shoulder."

Aileen narrowed her eyes and balled up her hands, ready to sock her brother in his nose when her Da appeared beside him. "Go with the eejit, lass. I'll take care of the man he brought ta meet ya."

She relaxed her hand, but not before letting Edwin know just how displeased she was. "I'll meet yer friend, but I will not be courting the man. Ye best get it out of yer head right now that you have any say over my life. I've taken care of myself, Da and our sisters ever since Mam died, and you left us. So you have no right to decide for me about anything."

Then she pushed past him and walked down to the dining room where she knew the man would be waiting. Sure enough, sitting at the table nearest the stairs was a man with shaggy brown hair and an equally unkept beard. She was several feet from him, and she could already smell the sheep odor that wafted from him. Edwin had to be out of his mind if he thought this was a man she should allow to court her. He hadn't even stopped to clean up before asking for an introduction.

She sighed as he stood when she came into sight of him from where he sat. As she got closer, she realized that the man was a good three inches shorter than her and had to look up at her. She was going to murder her own brother for this humiliation. "I take it you are Mr. MacGregor, my brother's travel companion?"

"Aye lass, I am and yer brother didn't do you justice. Ye'll make a man want ta come home overnight, now won't ye."

She gasped at his forwardness. Obviously, this man spent too many nights out with his sheep and none learning proper courting manners. "I'm sorry, what did ye just say to me?"

The man scratched himself in places not proper with a woman standing before him, then smiled, showing his missing and decayed teeth. "I said ye'll do. What say we skip all this courting and go see if we can rouse the reverend and get this hitching done. That way we can get right to work on you providing me with several fine Scottish sons to help on my spread?"

Aileen looked up as her brother finally came down the stairs and spoke up so that he was sure to hear her. "Let me get this straight, Mister MacGregor. Even though we met all of five minutes ago, you want me to come with you to rouse the Reverend out to marry us now so that I can start working on bearing you several sons to work your spread with you?"

The man scratched himself again "Aye lass, are ye hard of hearing? I know yer a bit long in the tooth. But ye brother assured me ye were a fine specimen of a woman. What other prospects do ye have besides me? Ain't no reason to stretch this out when we both know I'm yer last hope of a husband and a family."

Aileen turned to say something to Edwin when she saw Millie come in from the kitchen. She turned to her sister-in-law instead. "Millie, have you met Mister MacGregor yet? Edwin brought him to court me; it seems."

Millie nodded, "Aye; I was there when they ran into each other."

"Well then, I'm sure it will please you to know that Mister MacGregor just informed me we should go see Reverend Theodore and get hitched tonight. All so I can get started on producing strong Scottish sons for him. After all, it isn't like a woman my age has any other prospects."

Millie's mouth dropped open. "He didn't!"

"Aye, he did. I wonder how Mister MacGregor feels about the new law giving women the right to vote and own property of their own? Tell us, Mister MacGregor, your thoughts on the women's rights law."

The man slashed through the air with his hand angrily. "Pure foolishness. No woman of mine will be voting or owning property. It isn't right, goes against God's very plan for our world."

"Does it now? Isn't that interesting, Edwin? Your good friend here thinks it's against God's plan for women to vote or own property. I wonder how he'd feel if he knew your own bride, the Reverend's sister, led the March through Creede asking for men to vote for that law? Or that you yourself marched and piped the parade to support that law."

She turned to see Edwin's face turning red, as was Millie's. "I'm sorry you came all this way for nothing, Mister MacGregor, but I won't be accompanying you to the church tonight or any time. You see, I'd rather be without a single prospect than marry a man who denies me my equality or thinks I'm only good for raising sons. I'm sure Edwin will show you to a room for the night. Ye'd best be getting back to yer sheep tomorrow morning."

"Now jest a minute, lass. Yer brother done gave me his permission, and we will be married."

"No, Mister MacGregor, we won't. You see that law you don't like gave me control over my life. My brother has no say over me. I have say, and I say that yer sheep will grow wings and fly before I marry the likes of you." She stopped in front of her brother.

"Edwin, you made this mess, I expect ye to see it set right. Goodnight ta ye all. Millie, I'll be down to help with breakfast."

Millie tried not to laugh out loud. She smiled with tears of laughter in her eyes. "Goodnight, Aileen. We can talk tomorrow."

"Aye, sounds good."

She climbed the stairs to hear her brother and MacGregor having words. She shook her head. "Well Da, ye better make sure he goes on his way tomorrow then."

She heard a chuckle beside her "Aye, lass, his foreman will arrive to tell him they lost one of his rams in the morn."

She locked her door behind her and quickly changed before crawling into bed and falling asleep dreaming of Sterling McCormick's sweet kisses.

Wednesday afternoon, Sterling stood beside the jail watching the door to the Hearth and Home, waiting for Aileen to appear. His second outing with her was about to start.

The couple of days since their first outing to the tea shop had been busy ones. He'd put a crew on his house and started work on the Irish pub for Paddy McGlynn. Aedan was heading up the crew and he knew his friend was a bit overwhelmed with his wife as well, but the job was a simple one. Rather straightforward, something the builder could handle with the plans they'd laid out.

Jake Honeycutt had agreed to do some of the inside woodwork for that job, as well as at Sterling's own house when they got that far. He wanted the hand-carved mantle over the main parlor fireplace repaired, and when he'd showed it to Jake; the man had told him he could replace the damaged sections and no one would ever know the difference.

He was pulled from his thoughts as he saw the women he dreamed about every night coming across the street, heading right for him with a big smile on her face. He took her by the hands when she got to him and drew her back beside the jail into the dark walkway beside the building, hiding them from the eyes of those passing by on Main Street. When he bent to take her lips in a kiss, her arms came around his neck and she melted against him. Their lips moved together until both of them finally pulled back, panting for air.

He placed several light kisses across her jaw and neck before stepping away from her. Then he stepped up to the edge of the building, and making sure no one saw them, led her back out and onto the boardwalk. "That was some greeting, Mister McCormick."

He smiled over at her as she wrapped her hand around his arm. "Yes, Miss McRae, it was, and you gave as good as you got, I must say."

She grinned at him. "After kissing me like that I must insist that you marry me, sir. I'm not one to have my affections toyed with."

Sterling stopped and turned to face her. "I know you're kidding with me, Aileen, but just as soon as my house is ready for us to move in, I will be asking you to marry me. Make no mistake about my intentions."

She looked into his eyes before slowly nodding. "Don't wait too long, Sterling. Edwin has already tried to force me to court someone since our last outing."

"Then let's go tell your brother about us right now. I'll make my declaration to him in front of everyone in his dining room and he won't be able to continue to keep us apart."

He turned to direct her back to the Hearth and Home, but she dug in her heels. "No, not yet. He's still hurting over the dressing down both Millie and I gave him. The man he brought home was a complete and utter disaster. Dirty, smelly and only looking for a woman to give him sons and lots of them right now. When he admitted he didn't believe women should own property or have the right to vote, Edwin knew he'd messed up. I promise you Millie and I set him straight. I also made it plain that I, and only I, would have any say on who would come calling on me and whom I would marry. Let him calm down a bit, then you can confront him again if you must."

So they had gone to the hotel as he'd originally planned, and then he'd walked her over to the old Gladstone Manor that his men were restoring. Once there, he'd shown her the plans he'd found and asked her opinion on the interior. When he told her it was his and he was restoring it for them, she had gotten excited and made him show her what he could inside. She was kissing him in each room they couldn't be seen outside from. Her lips were swollen by the time they realized she needed to head back to the restaurant for supper service.

Unwilling to let her walk alone, Sterling escorted her right to the corner of the Hearth and Home like he had two days before. He once again pulled her between the buildings and kissed her senseless. This time, however, he got bold and walked her right up to the door and held it open for her and when she entered; he followed her.

He stopped just inside and waited for one of her sisters to come and show him to a table, and he had just gotten seated when a shadow fell over him. "What are ye doing here, McCormick? I told you to stay away from me sisters."

"I'm not here to see your sisters, Edwin. I came to have supper. You do still serve supper, don't you?"

"Not ta the likes of ye, I don't. Now get!"

"Are you telling me you aren't willing to take my money, McRae? I wonder how your partners will feel about that when they hear you're turning down paying customers because they, at one time, courted your wife."

Edwin growled and reached for him just as Millie came out of the kitchen and saw them. She rushed over with a smile. "Mr. McCormick, how good to see you. You haven't been in for a few days. I thought you'd decided you didn't like our food."

He stood and smiled at Millie. "Not at all, Mrs. McRae. I thought it best to give your husband a few days to calm down. Like most Scotsmen, he has decided to make a feud out of a simple misunderstanding. I was just informed my business isn't welcome here anymore."

Millie looked between her husband and him with her hands on her hips. "Edwin, that isn't true, is it? You didn't tell Mr. McCormick he wasn't welcome here, did you?"

"Aye, he's just here nosing around Aileen. I won't have it."

Millie glared at him. "Did he say he was here for Aileen?"

"Nay, he said he was here to eat."

"Then there you go. He's here to eat like everyone else sitting at these tables. Get back in the kitchen so we can start serving them their food."

She leaned closer to her husband and whispered so only the three of them could hear her. "The sooner he's fed, the sooner he'll leave, Edwin."

The cook sighed and then turned and stalked back into the kitchen. Sterling sat down as Millie turned back to him and smiled. "Don't think I don't know why you're here, Sterling. You and Aileen need to be careful for a while longer. Come for meals and I'll make sure she serves ya. But you need to not return her with swollen lips again, Mr. McCormick. Because if my husband even suspects you're sparking with his sister, heaven help ya."

Sterling nodded and thanked her before she headed back into the kitchen herself. The meal was delicious and over way too quickly, but he couldn't do what he wished and pull his pretty waitress into his lap and kiss her. He ate and smiled at even the few lingering touches he got and gave. They whispered plans for Saturday and he left, knowing that he was going to have to take her on a picnic, otherwise they wouldn't get time alone like they needed.

He sighed as he headed out to make plans. He needed to talk to some of the wives in town and get them to invite Aileen for supper, and him as well, so they could spend time together away from the prying eyes of Creede. Maybe the Clarks and the Honeycutts. Aedan and Kara as well. The last might not work, as Edwin knew he was good friends with Aedan. Still, he'd find ways to spend more time with Aileen, and eventually he and Edwin would have it out over the girl and who she would be marrying.

Four

Time passed as Aileen and Sterling continued to court without Edwin finding out. Several of the families in town knew of their courtship and had conspired to give them time alone, away from prying eyes and wagging tongues. Aileen knew Sterling chaffed at her restrictions and wanted to confront her brother. He wanted to tell Edwin what they were doing. Aileen wanted that too, but she was worried because all of her income and even her housing came from Edwin.

If he really was as upset as he acted every time Sterling ate at the Hearth and Home, then she might find herself in the same situation as she had in Scotland. No income and no place to lay her head. While she knew if that happened, Sterling would marry her right then. She didn't want to have to marry him to make sure she was provided for. She wanted to marry him because they couldn't stand to be apart.

Not just between them had things changed. Reverend Bing and Celeste had grown to love each other, and when Archie Grady tried to kidnap the pastor's wife, he'd ended up running from the law and died under the wheels of his own silver cart.

The pastor and Celeste had opened a home for those women who had been abducted and any soiled dove who wanted out of the life, or any woman in need. Aileen helped Celeste and Millie with the women, teaching sewing and cooking to help supplement the lessons they got from the onsite teachers. She figured if Edwin tossed her out, she could always move in there until she and Sterling married.

Nathan Ryder had come to town to help his friend, the new furniture maker, with a shooting wager running one of the last outlaws out of town and bringing three others to justice with a six-gun.

The biggest change of all came when her own sister Rhona had quit working for Edwin and started working for the local newspaper owner. Even more surprising was when it turned out the man asked to court and then marry her. Almost as surprising was the fact that her sister had been writing western novels that the paper was publishing.

She had been instrumental in helping expose a Mail-Order Bride con that had fleeced several of the men in and around Creede. Aileen had been so proud of her sister for moving forward in her life. However, she would admit to herself she was jealous of the fact that her brother had approved of Mr. Carroll's courtship while her own had to be kept secret from him.

All that went through Aileen's head as she fought with her sister about the dress she was going to wear to work today. It took three tries before they got her sister to put on her best dress before leaving for the newspaper office. Rhona had complained all the way out the door about getting ink on her best dress and ruining it.

But Mister Carroll had come to her and Isla the day before and asked for their help in surprising her sister with the biggest wedding Creede had ever seen. The woman who had conned the men of Creede had promised a big wedding and community celebration dance at the Tivoli Ballroom. Mr. Carroll had paid for the reservation instead and planned to surprise Rhona with the wedding and dance today.

So now that her sister was out of the restaurant, her family closed down the shop and rushed over to the ballroom to be on hand to surprise her. Again, Aileen's heart burned with jealousy as her brother gathered the lace veil she and Isla had bought from Vivian Morgan for Rhona. He was going to walk her down the aisle and yet Aileen couldn't even sit with the man she loved for fear her brother would cause a scene.

Something had to give. Maybe Sterling was right, they just needed to tell him they were courting and let the chips fall where they would. The stress from having to keep her love and joy a secret was making her angry at her brother.

While Edwin was fussing over Rhona, Sterling slipped up beside her and whispered in her ear. "Save your dances for me tonight, sweet Aileen."

She looked at him and shook her head. "We can't, Sterling, you know that."

He smiled. "We can and we will. Even Edwin wouldn't risk ruining your sister's wedding reception."

She looked into his eyes and saw the determination there. "If we do this, there is no going back, Sterling. He'll know we've been seeing each other."

"What better place to let our intentions be known than at your sister's wedding, Aileen? The house will be finished soon and then we will have our own wedding. I'm tired of sneaking. I want to walk with you, arm in arm, and let everyone know you are mine. Don't you want that?"

She bit her lip in fear before nodding to him. "Alright, I'll dance with you. Then when everything is finished with Rhona, we will talk with Edwin. I just hope you're right and he doesn't make a scene."

"Either way, love. Today I am declaring my intentions to your family and our friends. I'm done hiding."

She sighed and entered the building, knowing that he'd slip to the other side to keep the peace until after the wedding at least. Her heart was in her throat the entire wedding ceremony knowing that during the dancing part of the night Sterling McCormick was going to make it plain to everyone that she belonged to him heart and soul. She said a quick prayer that Edwin would see that they were right for each other and leave his petty feud behind for her happiness.

Sterling sat at the table with the Clarks and Honeycutts for the wedding supper. "So, McCormick, I heard a rumor that you plan to let Edwin know your intentions to his sister tonight."

He looked over at the smiling face of Marta Clark. "Yes ma'am, I think my intentions will be known by one and all by the end of tonight."

The woman giggled before sobering. "While I am all for daring declarations of love, what are you going to do if Edwin reacts as badly as he did when you first approached Aileen at church?"

Sterling sighed. "I'm hoping that he realizes that I'm serious about this by now. I eat every meal at his place. While I've never come right out and made a declaration, surely by now he knows she has been walking out with me."

"I'm not sure he does, Sterling," Jake said. "From what I've heard, he's still looking for a man willing to court her. He mentioned the other day to KC he didn't understand why none of those miners who got swindled wouldn't agree to court her. He has no clue that everyone but him knows she is already courting you."

Just then the band started to play, and couples were moving to the dance floor. "Well then, I guess it's time he realizes just how serious I am. If you all will excuse me, I promised my lady I'd dance with her tonight."

He stood and walked right up to the table where Aileen sat beside Millie and Isla. "Aileen, may I have the pleasure of this dance?"

Edwin started to stand, but Millie put her hand on his arm. "Let's dance, husband." She clamped his arm with her hand and pulled him from the table to the dance floor. His eyes locked on Sterling and Aileen.

Aileen placed her hand in his and let him lead her to the other side of the dance floor. "You know she won't be able to keep him occupied all evening, don't you?"

"I know love, but it's time. He needs to see how we feel about each other."

She moved into his arms and before the first dance was done, she'd pressed in close and wrapped her arm around his neck. Her head was resting on his shoulder as they danced. He pulled her closer than was appropriate and she settled in to him, knowing they were made to fit together. As the music played and they danced, everything else seemed to fade away until it was just the two of them gliding across the dance floor, lost in each other.

When the fourth dance started, Sterling looked up at a tap on his shoulder to see one of the ranch hands from the Morgan's ranch standing there. "Mind if I cut in, partner?"

"I do actually, Miss McRae has promised all her dances to me, I'm afraid."

The cowboy looked confused. "But I was told to come cut in."

Aileen looked at the man then. "Well, you go tell my brother that I don't want anyone cutting in."

She laid her head back on Sterling's shoulder and he knew they were pushing Edwin and he'd respond soon. "You know he's going to come over here himself, don't you?"

He looked down at her "I know; are you ready for that?"

"Aye, you're right; it's time. He needs to know we won't give in to his bullying ways anymore."

When the song ended and the next one started again, there was a tap on Sterling's shoulder. "I've been sent to rescue the lady from ya. Her brother says you've taken up too many of her dances already."

"You can tell her brother that I'll release the lady when she asks me to and not a moment sooner."

The miner sighed. "I was told to not take no for an answer."

Aileen again looked the man in the eye. "You go tell my brother I refused to dance with anyone other than Mr. McCormick, and that's all there is to it."

"Are you sure, ma'am? I was told that you would be grateful to get away from his clutches."

"I am very sure, sir. I'm right where I want to be with whom I want to be there with."

The miner nodded. "I apologize then."

He walked away and Aileen and Sterling watched him make a straight line to Edwin who stood on the edge of the dance floor scowling at them. After a few angry words, Edwin started stalking toward them. "Get ready, love; your brother's on his way."

Just then Edwin grabbed his arm and yelled so loud the music came to a stop. "Let go of my sister, McCormick, and leave! I warned ye about messing with her."

"I will not let go, nor am I leaving, McRae. I plan to keep dancing with the woman I'm courting as long as the music is playing and the dance floor is open."

Edwin glared at him. "What game are ye playing at? My sister isn't courting ye. She isn't courting anyone."

"No, Edwin, you're wrong."

Aileen looked at her brother, "Sterling and I've been courting since the first week I arrived here. Everyone but ye and our sisters know it to be true."

Her brother's eyes flashed with anger and his face turned as red as Aileen's hair. "How could ye court this man? Ye know what I told him. Ye know he was supposed to stay away from ye and our sisters."

She stepped away from Sterling and faced her brother, and Sterling was worried now for her safety. "Who gave ye the right to decide who I can court? Hmm? I'm a strong independent woman with rights, brother. Ye have no say in who I court. Ye have no say in who I'll marry either, and if he asks then I'll marry Sterling McCormick as well."

"I'm the head of the Clan McRae, that's who I am, and as long as ye wear our tartan and live under my roof and work for our family, ye'll do as I say."

Now he turned his anger on Sterling. "This is all your doing. Ye couldn't stand that Millie married me, so ye had to cause discord in me family. I should beat ye senseless for this."

Sterling looked at Edwin with shock on his face. "Is that what you honestly think? That I'm courting your sister to get even with you for Millie? Are you daft, man? It was obvious at the March that Millie was going to marry you and I stepped back then, you eejit. I've not been playing false with your sister. I knew the moment I saw her at your wedding she was the one for me. I told her and everyone who would listen that I'd court her and marry her. The only person refusing to see the truth, boyo, is you."

"Ye're lying. Ye've no intention of marrying anyone. All one has to do is look at yer past to know that."

Sterling shook his head. "You're a fool, Edwin McRae. You don't even know what you're talking about. No intention? Is that what you said to me? Well then, tell me what this is?"

Sterling turned to face Aileen and sank to one knee, reaching into his jacket pocket and pulling out the ring he'd carried since the trip he'd taken to the mercantile back on the first day she'd agreed to court him. "Aileen McRae, will you do me the honor of becoming my wife?"

Edwin roared. "Don't you accept, Aileen, I forbid it!"

She looked at her brother, eyes flashing with anger. "Ye forbid it! Ye forbid it? Who are ye to forbid me anything, Edwin McRae? I helped raise ye. I watched ye sail away without a thought to me, our Da or sisters after Mam's death. I alone took care of our family. I alone watched our sisters grow to be fine women. I alone cared for Da as he lay dying. I alone stood up to the Laird when he demanded I become his mistress, and I alone took care of our sisters when he turned the entire village against us. Where were ye then to forbid anything? Ye sent for us when ye needed help. Well, ye can't forbid me anything. I alone will decide who I'll marry."

"If ye say yes to him, then ye'll not set foot in my house or restaurant again, lass."

Millie gasped, "Edwin, you go too far!"

Aileen turned away from her brother and reached out her hand. "Aye, Sterling McCormick, I will marry you."

She took his ring and put it on her hand. "Can you take me to my brother's business to collect my things? I'll be needing a ride up to Bachelor as well."

Millie looked at Aileen. "No, Aileen, you can't."

Aileen looked at her sister-in-law with tears in her eyes. "Aye, I can and I will, Millie. I knew it might come to this, and I've already talked to Celeste. I have a room in Celeste's House until Sterling and I wed."

Marta Clark stepped out of the crowd that had been watching the scene play out. "That's unnecessary, Aileen. You'll come to work for me starting right now. You can help me with the children and the house until Mr. McCormick's home is ready for you two to marry and move into."

Edwin glared at everyone. "No, I refuse to allow this, do ye all hear me?"

Aileen looked at her brother with sadness in her eyes that Sterling wished he could take from her. "Don't ye understand yet, brother? Ye have no say in this. Instead of being happy for me, ye've chosen to destroy what was left of our family. Over jealousy of a man who courted your wife for a few days. Who did the honorable thing and stepped back when she chose ye. Instead, ye try to destroy my chance at the same love and happiness ye found."

She turned away and pulled her sisters into her arms, who were weeping openly. "I love ye Isla, and ye Rhona. I'll see ye around town and at church, I'm sure."

Her sister nodded and clung to her before falling into Millie's open arms. "Thank ye for your friendship, Millie. I'll see ye around."

Then she turned to Sterling and wrapped her arms around him. "Mister McCormick, that ye need to seal our engagement with a kiss before I leave with my new employers."

"Whatever you want, Aileen." He wrapped his arms around her and kissed her like they were alone. When he came up for breath, she placed a hand on his cheek. "Come see me tomorrow after supper. We'll take a walk around the Circle C."

"I'll be there, love."

Sterling and the Clarks escorted her out of the ballroom. At the Clark's wagon he lifted her up after another quick kiss and headed home, wondering if he did the right thing in forcing this confrontation.

Five

Almost a month had passed since Aileen and Sterling had gotten engaged. She was settled into the routine at the Circle C ranch, helping Marta with the children and the kitchen so she could concentrate on caring for the twins. What Aileen thought had just been a job offered to give her a way to get out of moving into Celeste's House, turned out to be a very necessary position the Clarks had been trying to fill for several months.

While Sterling worked hard to get their house finished so that they could be married, he still stopped every day long enough to come and court Aileen. They'd gone on many walks around the ranch after supper as the sun was setting. They'd gone into both Creede and Topaz for dinner at the various restaurants, with one obvious exception. She and Sterling even had been invited to a few meals at Rhona's home, allowing Aileen to visit with both her sisters.

They filled her days with children and laughter, her evenings with courting and kisses that grew sweeter and more passionate with each passing day. Her nights were filled with dreams and with anguish. Dreams of her handsome fiancée and the life they would have together. Dreams of children of her own, yet anguish at the fact that her brother wouldn't relent.

The highlight of her week was Tuesdays when the ladies got together at the tea shop for tea. Her sisters had taken to staying afterwards to have some time alone with her. Isla had told her, and Millie had sort of confirmed it one week, that Edwin was a bear to live with. He snapped at everyone and was becoming a bitter and hateful man. He wouldn't even allow her name to be mentioned, and he'd made it plain that no one was to have anything to do with her or Sterling.

She couldn't understand how he could let something like jealousy take root in his life when he had so much to be happy about. He refused to be happy, instead becoming filled with bitterness and anger.

Not only had he forbid Millie and Isla from mentioning her name or Sterling's, any customer he overheard asking about them was told to leave the restaurant and not come back. Aileen was afraid that he was going to end up losing his dream because there was no way the Fontaine's were going to allow him to run the Hearth and Home into ruin.

Edwin's dream had always been to run a successful restaurant, and his cooking was good enough to guarantee that. But almost as important as wonderful food was good, friendly service. She knew all she could do at this point was pray for her brother's heart to soften. That and continue to plan her own future.

Today was Tuesday, and she sat in the tea shop with Marta as others came in. It thrilled them all when Celeste came in with Rachel and asked Regina for ginger tea and gingersnaps. They all knew what that indicated.

Millie heard her sister-in-law order the stomach calming drink and snack and squealed, "Oh Celeste, is it true? Are you carrying my brother's babe in your womb?"

The lovely pastor's wife blushed. "Yes, Doctor JT just confirmed it a few minutes ago. I haven't told Callum yet."

Millie laughed. "You may want to hold off on that for as long as you can, Celeste. You think Cal is protective of you now. Just wait until he finds out you're with child. He won't let you step out of the bed, let alone the house."

Celeste shook her head. "No, your brother is much more sensible than that, Millie."

Seffi Morgan laughed at that. "Oh, don't you believe it, Mrs. Bing. Ain't no man sensible when it comes to their woman being with child. Why I had to send for my mother-in-law when I told Waylon's father I was with child. The man refused to let me do anything. It got better with the other two, but not by much. You just wait and see, Celeste. That husband of yours will try to wrap you in cotton and keep you from doing even the most basic of things."

"Speaking of being with child, has anyone heard from Benita Theodore lately?"

Rachel spoke up. "Doctor JT has her on complete bedrest. She is having a lot of trouble carrying her child."

"I hope Reverend Theodore is treating her well."

Celeste cleared her throat. "I can speak to that. Believe it or not, I think Benita's troubles are helping to calm the Reverend and bringing out a more caring side of him."

"What makes you say that, Celeste?"

"Well, for starters, he came to see Callum and I Saturday night. He wanted to apologize for the way he treated us when we first married. He said he was preparing for his sermon and realized he couldn't stand before his congregation without making things right with us."

The ladies all exclaimed over that statement. Celeste nodded. "He was sincere. If that wasn't shocking enough, he asked if one or more of the girls in Celeste's House would come and help with Benita throughout the week. He seems genuinely concerned for her comfort and condition."

"Well, will wonders never cease?"

Seffi turned the conversation. "Okay ladies, I have a concern. We still have all those men who wanted mail-order brides and believed that phony matchmaker, Mrs. D'Arcy, was going to help them. Those men deserve wives. I say we need to work with them and help them find suitable matches. Of course, before we send for a trainload of mail-order brides, we need to make sure those men will make good husbands. I want to teach them how to court a lady. Can any of you help us with that?"

Aileen knew that the conversation went on from there, but she couldn't concentrate on anything. All she could think about was that soon Sterling's house would be done. Mr. Jorgenson would have their furniture made, and they'd be married.

Yet if her brother kept up the way he was, two-thirds of her family wouldn't be there. As it was, if she were to become with child, that babe would grow up not knowing his or her uncle and maybe not even one aunt.

Was she making a mistake in agreeing to marry Sterling? She loved him and couldn't see herself married to anyone else, but was it right to marry him and destroy her family?

When she looked up only her sisters, Millie and Celeste were left in the tea shop. The tea group was over and she'd not heard a word. Millie reached out and touched her hand. "What are you thinking about, Aileen? You look so sad."

She looked at the four women sitting with her sisters, sister-in-law and the pastor's wife, and a tear leaked out of her eye. "Am I making a mistake agreeing to marry Sterling?"

"Oh honey, what makes you ask that?"

"Edwin."

Millie sighed. "Aileen, he'll come around, you just need to give him time. You know how proud your brother is. That's all this is; his pride is wounded. He'll get over it, you'll see."

"What if he doesn't?" she whispered. "The house will be finished soon and the furniture not far behind it. I don't want to marry without my family there to celebrate with me. I don't want to have children who never get to know their aunts and uncle. Maybe I should just end things with Sterling and move back to the boarding house."

Isla slapped her hand on the table. "No, Aileen, ye've given up so much for us over the years. Do ye think I didn't hear what ye said at Rhona's wedding about why the town turned on us? Ye deserve happiness. Ye deserve the love of a good man, and contrary to what Edwin thinks, Sterling McCormick is a good man and ye love him. Don't ye dare let go of love. Don't. Ye. Dare."

They pulled Aileen into a four-way hug and then when she had finished crying they all turned to see Sterling standing in the doorway. She saw the look on his face and knew he'd heard her question and her doubt. "Sterling!"

He came to the table and kneeled beside her. "I love you, Aileen McRae, and if you need to wait until your brother approves, then I'll wait for you. Because I can't let you go. You own my heart, love. Without you, life isn't worth living. If you need me to wait for Edwin to come around, then I'll wait; but just know every day without you is like death to me."

He kissed her and then stood and walked out, leaving her crying harder than ever. "Oh, what have I done? What should I do?"

Celeste looked at her. "Go after him, of course."

Aileen looked at each of the women sitting at the table, and they all nodded.

"Go," they each echoed and without a thought Aileen was on her feet racing out the door after the man who owned her heart.

Sterling sat at the polished bar in McGlynn's Irish Pub. "Give us a pint, will ya, Paddy?"

"Sure thing, Sterling." The owner and barkeep filled the mug with beer and sat it in front of the architect, watching as Sterling gulped the whole thing down. He slammed the empty metal mug back on the bar. "Give us another."

The barkeeper's eyes drew down in displeasure. "Slow down, boyo. You know this is a respectable pub, not a place for hard drinking. What's got you in such a state, my friend?"

Sterling stared into the new mug that Paddy set in front of him. "I don't want to talk about it."

The man nodded. "Problems with Aileen, then. Only two things drive a man to drink like you are. Work problems or woman problems, and since I know your work is going well, it must be Aileen that drove you in here like the hounds of Hades were on your tail."

"It's not Aileen that is my problem, it's that bullheaded brother of hers. How can I ask the girl to give up her family for me?"

"Ah! Still not willing to give you his blessing, then?"

Sterling laughed, but not in a pleasant way. "His blessing? The daft bugger has forbidden any mention of me or Aileen inside the restaurant. Millie and Isla aren't allowed to see her, talk with her, or even mention her. If they do, he goes off, and it's driving Aileen into a fugue I can't reach her in."

The bartender nodded. "Give the man time, Sterling. He's a proud Scotsman. We all know how those crazy highlanders are."

Sterling banged his hand on the bar. "Time, the bloody amadan has had months to get over his pride. God in heaven, he married the lass. Why must he make his own flesh and blood miserable now?"

"He's Scottish, boyo. You know how long they can hold a grudge."

Sterling sighed and drain his mug again. "That I do. I told Aileen today I'd not marry her while she's estranged from them. I told her I'd wait for her and I will, but I'll be gob smacked if I'll sit around here and watch her beg for his favor."

The bartender frowned. "What are ye thinking man?"

Sterling stood, a little unsteady on his feet from guzzling two pints on an empty stomach. "I'm going to take the next train to Cheyenne. Man out there wants me to take on a job designing and building a hotel. Think I'll go look at the job. That will get me away for a while. Let me clear my head."

"You going to tell Aileen you're leaving?"

Sterling shook his head. "She's better off without me. Least then she can make peace with her family."

"That's wrong, Sterling; the lady deserves to know you haven't run out on her."

"I'll drop a letter off for John and Willie to take to her out at the Clarks after I leave. I promised to wait on her, Paddy, and I will. I didn't promise to do it in Creede."

"You're as much an amadan as you claim McRae to be if you run from this, McCormick. I thought you the better man in all this."

"I don't want to hear it, McGlynn's. What do you know anyway? You got your woman now, didn't ya?"

Sterling turned and stalked out of the pub. If he hurried, he'd be able to pack his bag and catch the last train of the night. He rushed to his house and tossed everything he'd need for several weeks into a carpetbag, scribbled a hasty note to Aileen letting her know he had business in Cheyenne and would be gone for a while for work. He sealed it and dropped it off at the mercantile on the way to the depot.

When the train pulled out that evening, Sterling was on it. He was heading to Cheyenne and Mr. Durant, who had wired him about planning and building a large hotel near the train depot. His heart, however, seemed stuck in Creede with a certain red-haired, blueish gray-eyed woman. He sighed. It's for the best.

Maybe this way she can reconcile with Edwin and be happy. Right on the heels of that thought was another one: a question he knew the answer to already. Would he be happy? No, but that was the price one paid sometimes for love.

Six

Aileen woke the next morning with a headache. She'd listened to the women and ran after Sterling, but he was gone. She'd looked for him everywhere she could think to find him, and he had been nowhere. Aileen had even asked Aedan Casey to check the Nugget and other saloons for her, but again nothing. She felt as if her heart was breaking along with the throbbing in her head. Aileen had been such a weeping mess when she returned to the Circle C, Marta had sent her to bed without letting her help with supper or anything.

Now it was morning and as she looked outside, she noticed it was a gray and overcast day, much like her mood. She dressed in her most drab day dress and just twisted her hair up in a bun at the back of her neck. She didn't even care to look nice in case Sterling came calling. Aileen knew he wouldn't. He'd made it plain that he'd give her space and time to decide what she wanted. His words still echoed in her head and the haunted, broken look on his face consumed her. "Just know every day without you is like death to me."

How could she have stabbed him in the heart like that? She should have grabbed him and told him she loved him, that she chose him. But she hadn't. She'd sat there as the man she claimed to love walked out the door and disappeared. She swiped the tears from her eyes and went to start breakfast. Marta would be busy nursing the twins and the other children would be up soon hungry. She sighed again. Life went on even when your heart is shattered, she realized. So she wiped her eyes again and got to work.

As the day wore on it was obvious to everyone, including the children, that something was upsetting Aileen. As they finished dinner, Marta sent the children to play in the house's backyard. "Stay close, you all. Aileen and I need to talk."

Rachel nodded "Yes Mama, I'll keep them close."

"That goes for you as well, Rachel. Don't wander or head to the stream; and stay close enough that we can see you and you can hear if we call you."

"Yes, Mama," they all said.

Once they were gone, Marta turned to her and pointed at the table. "Sit, I'll bring us some hot chocolate and then you can tell me what is wrong."

Aileen sat at the table, knowing that she would have no way out of telling Marta everything that happened yesterday after she left the tea shop.

Marta reached out and took her hand. "And did you?"

Aileen frowned. "Did I what?"

"Go after him?"

"Aye, but I dinna find him; it was like he vanished."

Now it was Marta that frowned. "How does a man Sterling's size just vanish?"

"I dinna know. I just knew that he was nowhere. I even asked his friends to check the saloons for me. No one has seen him since he left the tea shop."

Just then there came a knock at the door and Marta smiled. "Well, maybe that's him come to spark with his fiancée some more."

Aileen stood "Oh, I look a mess."

Marta laughed. "I don't think he'll care one bit, Aileen. Go answer the door. You don't want to keep him waiting."

Aileen nodded and rose, patting her hair and trying to make herself more presentable before she opened the door. She looked back at Marta, who indicated with a shooing motion that she should hurry. Aileen yanked the door open and her shoulders slumped. Standing at the door with an envelope in his hand was Willie Meeks.

"Hello Willie. Are you making a delivery? I don't believe we ordered anything from the mercantile this week."

The young man dragged the toe of his shoe across the porch. "No ma'am, Miss Aileen. A letter was left for you at the store, and Mrs. Toria asked John and me to bring it to ya on our deliveries."

The boy held out the envelope. "Thank you, Willie. Would you like a couple of cookies to take with you?"

"Oh no, ma'am, we're stoppin' at the Morgan's next. Mrs. Seffi will have some sandwiches and cake fer us."

"All right, then. Thank you and thank Toria for me."

The boy nodded. "Yes, Ma'am." He turned and ran back to the wagon where John sat, and the man pointed over the boy's shoulder and Willie stopped and spun around. "Oh and have a nice day."

Then he ran and hopped up beside John, who turned the wagon and headed back up the lane. Aileen stared at the envelope with her name on it. The writing was masculine, and she felt a ball of dread settle in her stomach.

"Who's it from?" Marta asked her. Aileen tore it open and pulled out the single page, reading the simple message written on it before wailing like death itself had come for her. The letter fluttered out of her hand and landed on the floor. "It's from Sterling. He left Creede last night, he's taking a job in Cheyenne."

She looked up at Marta. "What have I done? He didn't even say goodbye."

She ran to her room and threw herself on the bed, weeping for the love she'd let slip from her fingers.

It had been two weeks since Sterling had fled from Creede on the last train of the night. Mister Durant was a self-important man who knew what he wanted and how to get it. He'd shown Sterling the site where he wanted his hotel built.

Durant told Sterling that he wanted the biggest and finest hotel in all the West, with of course the exception of San Francisco.

"I want five stories and the finest of materials, McCormick."

Sterling nodded. "Of course, Mister Durant. You realize that with what you're asking for, the plans alone will cost you a fairly enormous sum, and it would take almost two years to build if I brought both my teams from Colorado and hired another skilled team here in Wyoming?"

"Cost is not object man, why the railroad was good to me. Draw up a contract and we'll get started."

Sterling hesitated. He'd only meant to be gone a few weeks. If he took this job he'd be away from Creede, away from Aileen for two years. He thought back to the pain in her eyes and voice as she cried out her heartache to her sisters, Millie and Mrs. Bing. She wanted her family, and Edwin would never consent to them marrying. He'd promised her he'd wait for her, and he would. There was no other woman for him, there never would be. He'd wait and work, knowing that she'd never be free to be his wife.

Eventually she'd go back to Edwin and the bullheaded Scot would find her a man he approved of. He couldn't stay in Creede and watch her marry some other man, he couldn't stand it. Yes, he'd wait, but he'd do it here in Wyoming for now. "Give me a week and I'll have a contract and tentative plans for you, Mister Durant."

The wide, well-dressed tycoon smiled. "Good man. I'll see you in my office in a week. Don't disappoint me now. I want the grandest design you can come up with."

Sterling shook the man's greasy, weak hand. "I'll do my best, sir."

The railroad tycoon turned and waddled away back to his highly polished black coach and waited as his driver opened the door and helped the man inside. Once they had driven off, Sterling turned and made his way back to the room he'd taken in a boarding house just past the center of town. His thoughts were not on the challenging project before him, but the women he'd left behind.

"Well, ye are as daft as Edwin, aren't ye laddie?"

Sterling jumped at the sound of the familiar voice and looked to his left to see the same old Scotsman in the same kilt walking beside him. He scowled at the man. "I'm nothing like that bloody wanker."

"Aye ye are, ye're like two peas in a pod, ye are. Both so proud ye be willing to let the best Scottish lass slip right through yer grasp. Him, his sister, and ye the woman God created jest for ye. All because ye both got yer feelings hurt."

"Leave me alone, old man, or so help me God I'm going to give you a beating you'll likely remember for years."

"Go ahead and take yer best swing, laddie. Duncan McRae never ran from a fight, and I refuse to start now."

"McRae? You're a McRae?"

"Aye, Duncan McRae of the Clan McRae."

"You've been playing me for a fool from the start then." Sterling roared and threw himself at the man, intending to knock him to the ground and delivering a beating once there. Only things didn't go as Sterling planned, as his roar turned into a yelp of surprise and he passed right through the older Scotsman. He found himself on his hands and knees in the dirt. I

f that wasn't humiliating enough, the man turned and laughed as he took his booted foot and shoved Sterling in the backside, sending his face into the dirt of the Wyoming street. "I told ye lad, yer as wool headed as Edwin. What made ye think ye could lay hands on an angel, anyway?"

Sterling spit dirt out of his mouth and spun to look up at the man. "An angel? You're an angel?"

"Well, not exactly. I'm filling the role of a guardian and guiding angel, but really, I'm Duncan McRae."

Sterling stood slowly and dusted himself off. "So God sent me a McRae to be my guardian angel."

The old man scratched his chin "Well actually I'm not assigned ta ye at all, lad. I'm assigned to the bonny lass. I couldn't leave her in the mess she got in when I passed on."

Sterling stopped and looked at the man, really looked at him. "Aileen? You're here for Aileen." He took a step forward "You look like an older, shorter version of Edwin. You're their Da, then?"

"Aye, lad, and ye are in the wrong place. Ye need to be in Creede in two days or it will be too late for her."

Sterling's shoulders slumped. "Edwin found her a husband, then?"

Duncan stepped close and slapped him on the back of the head. "Pay attention, lad. Aileen will never marry another man. She loves you. No, it's worse than that. If ye ain't in Creede in two days, then Aileen will simply disappear, and her body won't be found until spring. If ye don't save her lad, she's gonna die before her time."

"So, you go save her!"

"I can't now, can I? It's against the rules. Just like it would be against the rules for me ta tell ye that she's so distraught at not hearing from ye that she's going to go for a walk by the river where ye picnicked. Because she ain't paying attention, she won't realize that the snowmelt from the first snow has weakened the river bank. I can't tell ye she falls in and drowns, carried away by the current to the valley below Creede. Nor can I say that she won't be found until after the spring melt. But I can't tell ye that because it would break the rules, wouldn't it?"

Sterling grabbed the angel and shook him. "But you have to do something! I can't get there in two days. Even if the train left heading east right now, it would take three to get to Creede."

Duncan reached out and grasped Sterling's shoulders. "If ye could get there, would ye save her? Would ye pass up this job and marry the lass?"

"Yes, I love her, you old fool. But you came too late, it's impossible."

"Ain't nothing impossible, lad. We jest need a slight miracle. Grab hold of me sash."

Sterling shook his head, "What?"

"Stop being a wool headed eejit, lad, and grab me sash!"

Sterling wrapped his hand around the tartan sash that crossed Duncan's chest and stumbled as he became dizzy with the movement that whirled around him. When everything steadied out, he was standing on a train platform a few feet from the ticket window. "Where are we?"

"Denver, that's two days from Creede. Get on the train, Sterling, and save my daughter!"

"Why didn't you just take me to Creede?"

"I told ye lad, I can't break the rules. Denver was stretching them as far as I could. Now get, before ye miss the train."

Sterling looked at the ticket window and then back to ask Duncan a question, only to realize he was alone again, hundreds of miles from where he started. He walked up to the window. "One to Creede, please."

"You just made it, Mister. The eastbound train leaves in about a minute."

"Then I guess you should give me my ticket. I've got to get back and see my bride."

Sterling handed the man his cash and took the ticket and settled into a seat. In his mind he sent a thought to Aileen, praying that she would feel his love and intent. "Hold on, love! I'm coming."

Seven

Aileen was still distraught two weeks later after the letter she received from Sterling telling her he was taking a job in Wyoming. In a moment of remorse and panic she had considered breaking their engagement and returning to the Hearth and Home to reconcile with her brother.

Sterling had heard her and told her he would wait for her to be ready to marry him no matter how long it took. And then he'd hopped a train to Wyoming to meet with one of the richest railroad tycoons in the United States to talk about building him a hotel.

Here she lay where she had for the last fourteen days. Knowing that he would be gone much longer than the few weeks he promised her if he actually took the job; she found she didn't have the energy to even get out of bed. Instead, she had retreated to her room and refused to even eat.

The door opened and Marta walked up to the window and threw open the curtains, letting the sunshine in. "This has gone on long enough, Aileen McRae."

"Leave me alone, Marta."

"No; I've allowed you to have your pity party, but as Scripture says for everything there is a season. A time to mourn and a time to rejoice. You've had your mourning; you may not rejoice, but you will not hide away in here feeling sorry for yourself. This is what is going to happen. You are going to get out of that bed and get clean clothes. Then you are going to go into the bathing room and get in the tub that has been filled for you, because frankly, YOU STINK!

While you bathe, I will air out this room and strip your bed. After you've washed and dressed in clean clothes, you will come out and have breakfast with me and the children. They are worried about you and need to see that you are alright.

"After breakfast you will help them with their lessons and when that is done you need to go into town. Mister Jorgenson sent word yesterday that the furniture for Sterling's house is ready and you need to show him and his men where to put everything."

Aileen gasped and sat up. "I can't do that, Marta, it's not my house."

"Poppycock! It is your house! Everyone who was at your sister's wedding knows Sterling said he was going to marry you as soon as they finished your house. It's your house and you need to tell the men where to put the furniture."

Aileen sighed. "Fine. But I don't know what good that will do. Sterling is still in Cheyenne and I have heard nothing from him since he left."

"So write him a letter!"

Aileen looked at her friend. "What?"

"You told your brother you were an independent woman, didn't you?"

"Yes." Aileen said with confusion in her voice

"Then act like one. Stop waiting to hear from Sterling. He's a man; they don't think about things like letters. Write him and tell him you didn't mean what you said. Tell him the house is ready and that you are ready for him to keep his word and come marry you."

"That will not work, I don't know where he is."

Marta shook her head. "You know that he went to Cheyenne to meet with Mr. Durant about building him a hotel, right?"

Aileen nodded. "That's what his letter said."

Then you send it to Sterling McCormick in care of Mr. Durant, Cheyenne, Wyoming. If he's working for Mr. Durant, I would assume that the man could get Sterling a letter. Once you write to him, he will probably write you back.," Marta grinned at Aileen, "Unless he hops a train and rushes back here to marry you instead."

Aileen wasn't so sure Marta hadn't seen his face when she talked about calling off their wedding. He may write her back, but then again he might still be upset with her. Either way, she needed to do what they expected of her. She'd get clean, help with the children, and get the furniture moved into his home. Then she'd think about writing to him.

One step at a time, she told herself. With that, she grabbed her clean clothes and headed for the warm bath waiting for her.

Sterling had been lost in his own thoughts since he got on the train in Denver. He prayed nothing delayed the train. He prayed that he'd be in time to save Aileen. Sterling even prayed that she would still want to marry him. He prayed that somehow he and Edwin could put aside their differences so that Aileen wouldn't have to choose between them. He was just getting ready to start his prayers over from the beginning when his attention was caught by a commotion at the front of the car.

An obviously pregnant woman was waving a ticket and arguing with the porter. "It couldn't be helped, I tell you. My brothers were sick, and it delayed us in Denver. I was told this ticket was good anytime."

The porter was nodding "Yes ma'am, it guarantees you a seat but not a private sleeper. We don't have any empty ones. The best I can do is offer you a seat here in this car. I'm sorry."

The woman's face crumpled. "But I'm with child, I need to be able to lie down and rest."

Sterling had a private sleeping berth. He'd been in such a hurry he hadn't even realized that the ticket agent had stuck him with the more expensive berth until an hour after they got underway when the conductor offered to show him to his berth. He hadn't been tired, so he told the man he'd retire after supper. Now he knew why he'd had the berth. Because this woman needed it.

He stood and walked up to the porter. "Excuse me, I have a private berth, C7."

The porter looked relieved to not have to deal with the woman for a few minutes. "Yes sir, berth C7, that's in the third car from the locomotive. Shall I show you to your berth, sir?"

Sterling shook his head. "No, you misunderstand me. I'd like to offer the lady my berth. I believe she needs it more than me."

The porter shook his head. "I can't do that, sir; that berth was sold to you, not her."

"I don't think you're getting my intentions, mister. I paid for that berth, correct?"

"Yes, sir."

"Then if I want the lady to use it to rest, I can do that, correct?"

The porter thought about it. "I don't see why you can't, sir. As you said, you paid for it. But I won't have another one for you, sir."

"That's alright, I don't mind sitting up for a day. I can sleep almost anywhere and I'm only sleeping for one."

"Thank you, sir. I don't know how I can repay you."

Sterling smiled at her. "Unnecessary, ma'am. I couldn't help but overhear your conversation," he said as he escorted the woman toward the sleeping berth. "You said you were traveling with your brothers and they got sick?"

"Yes, I had to leave them in Denver. They both will return home after they're well."

"Well, I'm glad I could help. Now you rest here and when you wake, why don't you come sit with me in the common car. I'm not your brothers, but I promise I'll see that you aren't accosted, at least until tomorrow, when we get to Creede. That's where I'm getting off."

"Oh! Me too. Do you know a Reverend Bing?"

"Yes ma'am, I sure do. I know Callum, his wife Celeste, and his sister, Millie. Why?"

The woman looked around to make sure no one was near. "I was supposed to arrive last week, but with my brothers sick we got delayed. I need to get to Reverend Bing. A friend of mine arranged for me to stay at Celeste's House until my baby comes."

"Ah! Well, I know several people that could help you get to Celeste's House. I'd take you myself, but I have an appointment shortly after I arrive. I'm Sterling McCormick, by the way."

"Oh, how rude of me, I'm sorry. I'm Carol Brown."

"It's a pleasure to meet you, Mrs. Brown. I promise I'll see you safely to Creede and arrange for someone to take you to Celeste's House as well."

"Thank you, Mister McCormick; you've been a real Godsend."

"Glad to help, ma'am. You get some rest now. I'll see you later this afternoon."

"Yes, thank you again."

He smiled and walked away. "Think nothing of it, Mrs. Brown."

Eight

Aileen climbed out of bed the next morning, still feeling down and confused. She knew Marta was right. She needed to write to Sterling. He had told her he'd give her time and space to decide when she wanted to marry him. If she didn't let him know, he might stay away for quite a while. But what did she say? Yes, she wanted to be his wife, even if it meant never reconciling with her family. Yet at the same time, she wanted Edwin and Sterling to make things right. On top of that, how did she ask Sterling to come home and marry her when he'd be giving up what had to be a very profitable project?

She, like everyone, had heard of Mr. Durant and knew that he was very wealthy. If he asked Sterling to come design a building for him, he had to be paying top dollar. She'd be proud to be the wife of a man in such high demand. A hotel probably wasn't a small project. It would take a long time to build, and her home now was in Creede. Was it fair to ask him to come home and marry her now and give up that project?

She needed time to think of what to say and how to say it. Aileen needed to decide if now was the right time for them to marry.

Perhaps they should delay marriage until he finished this project? Maybe those were the decisions they should make together.

Aileen knew what she'd do, she'd pack some stationary and a pen and inkwell into a saddle bag. When the younger children went down for their nap, she'd see if Marta would mind if she took a ride down by the river. She'd go to that special spot Sterling had shown her on the one and only picnic she'd been able to talk him into going on with her.

She couldn't help but smile at his nervousness as they rode out to the hidden clearing beside the river. He explained his history with disastrous picnics and she had laughed all the way to the spot. Thankfully, their picnic had been without disaster and the passionate kisses they'd shared had helped Sterling overcome his fear that picnics were cursed for him.

Yes, that's what she'd do, go walk down in their secret spot and figure out what to write him. But first she needed to get back to work doing the things the Clarks paid her to do. Helping Marta with chores and her abundance of children.

Sterling's thoughts were conflicted. Aileen's Da had been so adamant that he needed to get to Creede in two days' time or Aileen would die. He'd told him how she'd die, but not where along the river she'd fall. How was he supposed to save her if he didn't know where she'd be?

Then he also had promised Mrs. Brown that he'd see her safely to someone he trusted to get her to Celeste's House and Reverend Bing. How was he going to do both things?

If nothing else, he could take Mrs. Brown to the telegraph office and put her in Arthur and Beatrice Jameson's care. He knew they would help. They were firm supporters of Reverend Bing, and Arthur was one man on the courtship committee of Celeste's House. With that decided, he turned his thoughts back to Aileen.

Where would she go to think along the river? The only spot he could think of was the hidden clearing he'd shown her where they had their picnic. He couldn't help but smile at the way she'd teased him about all his picnic disasters before theirs. He also couldn't stop before remembering how they had kissed and the passion that had almost gotten away from them beside the river.

Carol Brown interrupted his thoughts. "You must really love her."

He looked up, confused to be sitting on the train beside the pregnant widow when the memories of Aileen had seemed so real. "The look on your face just then. You were thinking about your fiancée, weren't you?"

"Yes, I was."

"She's a very lucky woman to be loved like that. I'd give almost anything to have someone look at me like that just once."

Sterling shook his head. "I'm the lucky one, Carol. Lucky that she is willing to marry me. Don't give up; you could still find a love like that. I told you some of my story. Aileen isn't the first woman I attempted to court. There were a few others as you know. But in comparison, they were all wrong. You could still find that man who will love you beyond compare."

She shook her head. "I doubt it, not after the baby comes. Most men don't notice a woman with a child."

"Well, I'll keep praying that the one God created for you will come along to help you with your new start. I know this: where you're going, that baby, and you will be loved, and that baby spoiled. You just wait and see."

She smiled a nervous smile "I hope you're right. I'm just glad Fiona knew about this place."

"Well, she should. She was sent out by them to her new start as well."

"I think I knew that. I think she told me that before giving me my ticket."

Sterling opened his mouth to reassure her again when the conductor walked into the car. "Next stop, Creede, Colorado. Creede, next stop."

"Well, Mrs. Brown, it's time to take that first step to your fresh start and for me to take the next step to my marriage. Are you ready? I know I am."

She stood and took his arm in one hand and her carpetbag in another. "I am, Mr. McCormick, again thank you for your generosity and protection."

"Least I could do, Mrs. Brown. Wish I could take you to Celeste's House and introduce you to Reverend and Mrs. Bing myself, but I have a pressing appointment."

She smiled at him as the train slowed to a stop at the depot. "I understand, Mr. McCormick I'm just grateful I ran into you."

Sterling directed her to the depot floor and looked up to see Millie McRae standing just a few feet away. "Oh, what luck. Come with me." He directed Mrs. Brown toward Millie. "Hey Millie, just the person I needed to see."

Millie frowned at the woman on Sterling's arm. "Sterling, I think you have some explaining to do."

Sterling chuckled. "This is Mrs. Brown. Fiona sent her to Celeste and your brother. I need to get going. Can you see she makes it to them safely?"

Millie's entire demeanor changed. "Oh! Mrs. Brown. Callum and Celeste were expecting you two weeks ago."

Sterling left the widow in Millie's capable hands and practically ran toward Otto's livery.

He tore through the doorway. "Otto, I can't explain, I just need your fastest horse and I need him now."

Otto nodded. "He's already saddled, Sterling. I was getting ready to exercise him."

"Thanks, I'll get him back to you as soon as I can."

Sterling vaulted into the saddle and kicked the gelding into a gallop. He flew out of the stable and headed out of town, pushing the horse as fast as it could go, racing death and praying he'd win.

Nine

Aileen almost missed the hidden path that led to the secluded clearing that Sterling had brought her to those few months ago. She thought it might have been because she was coming from the opposite direction from last time. But she had found the path and turned her mare down it. Sure enough, soon she was in the clearing where they had picnicked and talked and sparked.

She blushed as she thought about what had almost happened, how they both had gotten too carried away. Sterling's lips had been on hers and then along her jaw and her neck, and his hands had been working on the buttons of her dress when he jumped up and apologized. "I'm so sorry, Aileen, love. I almost got too carried away there."

She blushed even harder, thinking of her response. "I don't mind, Sterling."

He'd looked at her. "I do. I respect you too much to jump our vows, Aileen. When I take you to my bed, you'll be my wife, not before." He turned his head while she buttoned herself back up. When she stood and wrapped her arms around him he'd kissed her a few more minutes, then pulled away, blowing out a frustrated breath. "I'd better get you back to town before I make a liar out of myself."

He'd picked up the quilt and gathered up the picnic supplies, putting them all in the basket before offering her his arm. Sterling had walked her back to the buggy he'd rented from Otto. Then he'd kissed her once more and helped her up into the buggy. Taking her home with her virtue intact.

Aileen realized as she sat there looking out over the water, that was when she'd realized she loved him. Oh, he had caught her attention before that and he'd excited her before that. But right then when he refused to take what she would have freely given him because it wasn't his to take, that was when she knew she loved him.

She thought about Edwin and his repeated accusations that Sterling was nothing but a womanizing rake, a cad of the highest order. But she knew he wasn't. A rake would have known she was willing and taken advantage of her lapse in judgement. A Rake would have never once considering what it would have done to her reputation and prospects. Sterling had realized the temptation they were both about to succumb to and had removed them from it. Protecting her not only from his desires, but her own as well. With that thought, she knew exactly what to write to him.

She slid out of the saddle and pulled the stationary, pen and inkwell out of the saddlebag, and after checking the nib of the pen, filled its reservoir with ink and wrote.

My Dearest Sterling,

Thank you for writing and letting me know you had business out of town and would be gone a few weeks. I wish you'd told me in person so that I could have said goodbye and maybe kissed you. I understand why you didn't. I confused you as much as I confused myself.

What you overheard, my love, was not me trying to back out of marrying you. Just a woman torn between the man she loved and the family she had poured herself into for a lot of years. I came after you when you left, but I couldn't find you. I wanted to tell you then that I had chosen you, but you were gone.

I hope your business in Cheyenne is going well. I know Mister Durant would be lucky to have his hotel designed and built by you. Speaking of building, Mr. Jorgenson came to see me the other day. He wanted me to show him and his workers where to put our furniture.

As we'd discussed, I met them at the house. It's ready, my love, for us to move in. When you're ready to come home to me, I'll be waiting. Ready to walk down that aisle and say I do. Ready to become Mrs. McCormick, ready to be your wife. Hurry home to me, Sterling.

Your loving bride,

Aileen.

She placed the bottle of ink on the corner of the letter to hold it down while the ink dried, and she walked over to the edge of the bank, looking out over the river and up at the mountains beyond. Thinking of Sterling's lips on hers and wishing he was here to make her dream a reality. She heard a noise like a horse moving fast down the path behind her and turned to see who it was.

Suddenly the bank disappeared beneath her feet, and with a quick scream she plummeted into the icy depths of the fast-moving river.

Sterling worried as his horse blew hard as white foam flicked off his sides. He might end up having to buy Otto a new horse if he kept pushing this one. They were almost to the site of the picnic he'd had with Aileen. Sterling could feel the impending danger racing along beside him. He looked over and saw a dark figure on a pale horse racing alongside him.

Somehow he knew it was the angel of death. This was the race for Aileen's life and come hell or high water, Sterling would not lose. Not today. He kicked the gelding and leaned close over his neck, yelling in the horse's ear. "Just a little more, boy. We're almost there."

The horse responded as if he understood and Sterling glanced to his side, realizing he had pulled ahead of Death by half a length. He saw the path to the clearing and turned the horse at top speed.

They flew down the path, four hooves eating up the ground with Death falling further behind. As he broke through the clearing, he saw the top of Aileen's head. Her red hair shining in the sun over the back of her horse. She turned as if she heard him coming, and then she was gone with a scream and a splash.

Sterling turned his horse to run parallel with the river. He saw Aileen bob to the surface a few feet further down the river. The current was swiftly carrying her away at the same time the weight of her soaking wet dress was trying to drag her to the bottom.

Sterling kicked his mount again and again, and the horse responded with a supernatural burst of speed. They were pulling ahead of Aileen, who was struggling to stay afloat.

When they were half a horse's length ahead of her, Sterling pulled his right foot out of the stirrup and lifted it up on the saddle so he could pull off his boot. Then he did the same with the left. He tossed the boots over the side of the horse onto the ground, then spun so that he was sitting sideways in the saddle, both feet braced against the right side of the horse. He urged the mount closer to the edge of the bank and then, with a mighty push from both feet, launched himself off the horse and into a dive into the icy depths of the river.

He started up toward the surface when he saw Aileen sinking toward him. Sterling grabbed her around the waist, and kicking with his legs, drove them both to the surface. He quickly maneuvered them toward the bank and when his hand hit the bottom of the riverbed he quickly stood, picking Aileen up in his arms. "Sterling! Ye saved me!"

He smiled at her as his teeth chattered from the frigid water soaking his clothes. "That's right, love."

She frowned. "I'm so cold. Why am I cold, Sterling?"

"You fell in the river."

"Oh, that's right, I'm drowning."

"No love, I've got you."

She shook her head. "Ye can't have me. Ye're in Cheyenne. Yew wrote me a letter that said so."

"I know love, but I came back."

"I'm cold, Sterling, why am I so cold?"

"You fell in the river, love. Hold on, I see a cabin; I'll get you warm."

"Alright, I'm gonna go back to sleep now so I can keep dreaming about ye."

Sterling shook her. "No, Aileen. You have to stay awake."

"But I'm so tired."

"I know, love, but that's because you're so cold you have to stay awake for me."

"I'm cold, why am I so cold?"

"You fell in the river, love."

"Am I dead? I think I'm dead."

"You're not dead, love, I saved you."

"No, ye didn't, 'cause Ye are in Cheyenne. Ye wrote me a letter telling me so."

Sterling cursed; she was going into shock. He had to get her out of those wet clothes and get a fire started. Sterling strode up to the ramshackle cabin and kicked the door open. He marched over to a table and chair and sat Aileen down. "Get your dress off, Aileen."

She shook her head. "No Sterling, we aren't married. Ye can't do that yet."

"Not for that, love. Your clothes are wet and cold and they are making you cold. Get them off so we can hang them before the fire I'm making."

"Oh, all right. I'll do that after I take a nap."

Sterling dumped the load of kindling he found on the hearth in the fireplace and turned to Aileen, who was trying to climb up on the table. He pulled her to her feet. "Aileen, there's a bed over there, see it? Get your wet clothes off and then you can take a nap."

She smiled at him and nodded. "All right, Sterling."

She reached for her buttons, her finger shaking. "I can't make my fingers work. Why can't I make my fingers work?"

Sterling grabbed a Lucifer out of the tin on the mantle and struck it, setting the kindling ablaze. Then he quickly added several logs and prayed they'd catch as he turned back to see Aileen climbing back up on the table. "What are you doing, love?"

"I'm going back to sleep so I can keep dreaming about ye, Sterling."

He pulled her back down on her feet and kissed her. "I'm not a dream, love, I'm right here. Let's get you out of those wet things."

He reached for her buttons and realized his hands were shaking too hard to work the tiny things too.

He was about to scream when he remembered the folding knife in his pocket. He pulled it out and opened it, then slide it down the front of Aileen's dress, cutting the threads holding the buttons on the fabric. Then he pulled the dress off of her and let it fall at her feet.

Next, he spun her around and tried to untie her corset. The strings were tight and knotted, thanks to the water. Again, Sterling cut the strings and flung the wet garment away. He pulled her camisole over her head and then quickly cut the strings on her petticoats, watching them fall away.

Next he yanked her unmentionables off and picked her up. He carried her to the bed and placed her on it. Sterling pulled the blanket up over her.

He went back to the fireplace and added a couple more logs until the fire was blazing hot. Then he tore his clothes off too. He spread all of their things out so the heat could dry them. Once that was done, he climbed in the bed with Aileen and under the heavy wool blanket, wrapping his arms and legs around her, trying to warm them both up.

Slowly he watched as her lips and fingers went from purple to blue and finally to closer to their normal color. He felt the warmth flowing between them and watched as her breathing became deeper and slower. Then slowly Sterling's eyes drooped and before long he too dropped into a deep, restful sleep.

Ten

Edwin McRae stood in front of his cookstove. The skillet popping with bacon grease as he whisked the pancake batter to fluffy perfection. He tipped the bowl to pour the first perfect circle when he was startled by a voice he'd never dreamed he'd hear again.

"Laddie, ye're the biggest wool headed eejit that ever lived, ain't ye?"

He straightened the bowl before the batter could drip into the pan and pushed the skillet to a cooler part of the cooktop. As he turned around, he was proven correct as the short Scotsman stood just inside the door to the dining room. "Da?"

"Aye, lad tis ole Da. Yer Mam pops in for a visit and it's all smiles and sunshine. I pop in and tis disbelief and frowns."

Edwin shook his head. "Mam only came to help me and Millie connect to each other."

"Aye, and a right fine job of it she did, too. So why are ye so determined to keep me from doing as fine a job, lad? What did I ever do ta ye?"

Edwin frowned. "What are ye talking about, Da?"

"What am I talking about? What am I talking about? Well lad, I'm talking about Aileen, yer older sister. Who is lying in a broken-down shack freezing ta death because of ye."

"What do you mean, because of me?"

"Are ye the only one allowed to marry the mate HISSELF created for ye, lad? Didn't yer older sister deserve the mate HE created for her?"

"Aye, Da, of course she does."

"Then why, ye tell me, have ye been acting like the backside of a donkey, lad? What was it ye said? Oh wait, I remember. 'I'm Edwin McRae, head of the Clan McRae, and I forbid it!' Aye, that's what ye said. Oh, and 'As long as ye live under my roof and work fer my company, ye'll do as I say.'

Aye, that was what ye said. And all because ye're still jealous that the woman ye love went on a picnic with the man. So jealous, in fact, that ye couldn't stomach the thought of seeing him across the table at family dinners, or holidays, or special occasions. So jealous ye tried to set the bonny lass up with a rotten teethed, mule-headed sheepherder."

Edwin turned red and opened his mouth to deny it. "Shut yer gob spout, lad. I'm an angel now, jest like yer mam. I know what yer thinking. So now because ye couldn't let well enough alone, yer own big sister who loved ye and cared for ye from the day yer mam gave life ta ye is lying in that isolated cabin on the verge of meeting the death angel hisself. Because ye twisted her up so much she couldn't choose between the family she helped raise and the man HISSELF made jest for her. So her death, lad, that will be on your hands."

Edwin turned white. "What are ye talking about, Da? Where is Aileen and why is she dying?"

His Da glared at him. "Ye remember that ole fishing cabin of Mister Anders'? The one he let that Dougal and Wade characters stay in?"

"Aye."

"She be there freezing after falling in the river while trying to get her head and heart ta line up because of ye and yer 'I forbid it' nonsense."

Edwin ripped off his apron and headed for the door. "Where ye going, lad? "

"To save her."

"Why? It ain't like ye loved her, anyway."

He turned and looked at his Da with shock on his face "That's not true, Da. I love Aileen as much as I love meself."

"Nay lad, if ye loved her like ye say, then ye would have been happy she found the love of her life. Instead, ye proved yer love by forbiddin' her from marrying him."

Guilt slammed into Edwin. As much as he wanted to deny everything his Da accused him of, he couldn't. It was jealousy and a desire to punish Sterling McCormick that caused him to forbid Aileen from courting and marrying the Irishman. All because the man had dared to court Millie. He headed for the door again when his Da spoke up. "Might better take the Reverend with ye, lad. He's sitting in yer dining room."

"Why should I take him?"

"In case ye don't make it in time."

Edwin cursed under his breath as he pushed into the dining room. "Reverend Theodore. Ye got that fancy buggy with ye this morning?"

"I do, Mister McRae, why do you ask?"

"I need ta borrow it and ye need to come with me. It's a bit of an emergency."

The gangly young minister stood and placed his bowler hat on his head. "Then let's be off. Can you tell me how you know there's an emergency?"

"Ye wouldn't believe me if I did, Reverend. Let's just say I have special knowledge."

The young man looked at Edwin. "There seems to be a lot of that going around Creede these days."

"Aye, lad, if ye only knew."

Sterling woke to the wonderful feeling of Aileen in his arms. He knew he should get up and get dressed. Now that she was warm, what they were doing was obscene and improper. But he didn't want to get up. Not yet. Sterling wanted to sink into the feel of her in his arms, nothing between them. He needed to get dressed, and wake her and get her dressed, and have Doctor JT check her out just to be on the safe side. He'd come so close to losing her last night. Racing Death he'd reached her first and had to watch the dark angel stand in the corner until her lips returned to their normal color.

She obviously wasn't completely well as she was still asleep going on twelve hours now, he figured. Sterling sat up and was trying to figure out how to get out from under the blanket without waking Aileen when the door crashed open and Edwin McRae stormed in. He took one look at Sterling's bare chest and his sister's head and shoulders and roared. "What is the meaning of this?"

Sterling held up his hands "It's not what it looks like Edwin, I swear."

Edwin pointed at him. "It looks like ye and my sister are naked in bed together!"

Sterling paused at that. "All right, it is what it looks like, but I swear to you nothing happened. Your sister and I came here once for a picnic; not here, but up the river a way. I came back early and had a feeling she'd be there. We had some things to work out. When I arrived, the bank gave out and dumped her in the icy river.

I raced ahead of her and dove in, pulling her out. She was shivering and turning blue and I knew if I didn't get me and her warm, we'd both die. So I carried her to this shack, built a fire, stripped off our wet clothes to dry them and put us in bed under the covers to warm up.

"Between fighting the river and the warmth, we must have fallen asleep. I just woke before you stormed in and as you can see Aileen is still asleep."

Just then Reverend Theodore walked through the door. "Oh my, that doesn't look good at all, does it? Mister McRae, I believe Mister McCormick is telling you the truth."

Edwin nodded his head. "I do too, Reverend, but she's still ruined, isn't she? Even if he didn't touch her. It destroys her reputation."

"That is true. I suggest you wake her and both of you get dressed and then I'll have no choice but to marry you."

Sterling shook his head. "I'll marry her. Planned to anyway, so that's no problem, but obviously she's in no condition for a wedding right now. Let me take her back to the Circle C and get Doctor JT to come check her out. When he says she's fit to walk the aisle, I'll bring her straight to the church for you to marry us."

Edwin shook his head. "Nay, lad. Bring her home to the Hearth and Home. That way her sister can watch over her. I agree, when Doc says she's fit then ye will marry her. And God help ye if ye don't make her happy, McCormick."

"As God is my witness, Edwin, that's all I've ever wanted to do."

Three days later Aileen stood outside the door of the church at Creede. All her family and friends were inside waiting for her and Edwin to walk down the aisle.

"Ye feeling all right, lass? If not, we can wait a few more days, no one will mind."

Aileen smiled at her little brother. "Aye, I'll mind and so will Sterling. This is all I've wanted, Edwin, since I first saw him at yer wedding. Be happy for me."

He pulled her into a hug and kissed her forehead. "Aye, lass. I am. Now let's not keep the bloody wanker waiting."

She smiled. "Be nice."

"Aye lass, I will; who knows when Mam and Da might make an appearance."

She nodded. "Aye, its strange having them meddle in our lives even now after they've passed."

"Aye, it is. Just think, they'll probably gang up on Isla."

Aileen laughed. "Aye, probably."

Then the doors opened, and she was walking down the aisle. Edwin glared at Sterling as he placed her hand in Sterling's and then took a seat. Reverend Theodore took them through their vows and before long he looked at Sterling. "I now pronounce you man and wife. You may kiss your bride, Sterling."

Her handsome Irish architect smiled down at her. "With pleasure."

Then his lips met hers and just like every other time, everything else disappeared and they were alone in the world.

At the wedding supper, people kept asking them what they were doing for their honeymoon. Sterling would smile and say. "Tonight, we're going to be staying at Gladstone Manor, but tomorrow we're taking a train to Cheyenne. I have a contract to get signed."

However, there was something in his eyes that told Aileen he wasn't telling the truth. So as they climbed into the buggy he'd rented for the night, she asked, "What are we really doing for our honeymoon?"

He smiled. "Oh, part of what I told everyone was right. We are taking the train to Cheyenne tomorrow. However, I know our friends and family plan to shivaree us tonight, so we won't be at Gladstone Manor."

"Where will we be?"

"I thought we might visit that little cabin by the water where we first slept naked together. I want some better memories of that place."

She snuggled close to him. "Aye, that sounds perfect."

With that they headed off to the seclusion of that little cabin by the riverside where they spent the night reveling in their love for each other.

Epilogue

"What do you mean he's in jail? I have a contract for him to sign to build a hotel. I have the plans right here."

The sheriff shrugged his shoulders. "I don't know what to tell you, Mister McCormick. The U.S. Marshals hauled him off yesterday."

Sterling looked at Aileen and then back at the lawman. "What for?"

"Fraud and theft of government funds. Apparently he claimed to have laid more track for the continental railroad than he really did. They seized all his assets. I don't think you're going to be building any hotel for him here in Cheyenne."

Aileen patted Sterling's arm. "Thank ye, sheriff, we appreciate the information."

Sterling let her lead him away. "So now what?"

"Now we go back to our hotel and take advantage of that great gigantic bed, and then tomorrow we go home. It wasn't like you needed the money, Sterling. There's plenty of work in Creede for you."

"I know, but I wanted to build the best hotel in the West."

"Maybe someday, love."

Sterling sighed, "Maybe someday."

Aileen smiled as she watched her husband out of the corner of her eye. After everything they'd been through to become husband and wife, she couldn't get enough of looking at her handsome Irish husband. Even though she said nothing, she was positive that anyone who saw her watching him could tell that she absolutely Adored the Architect.

The End.

Books by George

You can find all of George's books on his Amazon author page.
https://www.amazon.com/George-H-McVey/e/B007E39QUG

Cowboys and Angels Series
Rescuing the Rancher
Hannah the Healer
Banking On Beth
Persuading the Preacher
Sweet on the Swede: A Ladies of Celeste's House Book
Adoring the Architect
Winning His Wife
The Adventures of Bob the Rooster

Redemption Tales Series

Redeeming Reputation
Redeeming Trail
Redeeming Grace
Redeeming Love
Redeeming Character
Redeeming Family
Cindy Ryder: Girl Detective: The Case of the Secret Admirer
Dorthy's Disasters: A Ryders Legacy Historical Book

Mail Order Brides of Sanctuary Series
The Pastor's Replacement Bride
His Brother's Bride
Her Quiet Nurturer
The Sheriff's Unexpected Family
Fiona's Fresh Start

Silverpines Series
Mail Order Marshal: A Brides of Beckham Novel
Wanted: Miller
Wanted: Engineer
Wanted: Family

The Phantom Horse Bridge Series

Phantom Origins
Phantom Politics
Phantom Child

Java Cupid Series

Java Muse
Java Harmony

Nugget Nate Books

Nugget Nate: The Holiday Adventures
Nugget Nate: The Penny Calling
Marshall, Texas Ranger: The Case of the Hidden Pasts

Other Fiction

A Bride To Herd
Rudolph's Runaway Bride
The Reject Rescue (Sequel to Rudolph's Runaway Bride)
The Princess Game
Her Hero: Next Door
Melody's Next Christmas: A Ryder's Legacy Book
Music Box Christmas
The Cowboy's Shoebox Sweetheart
The Secret Santa Romance
Seeking Mrs. Claus
Rise of the Champion
George's Shorts

Nonfiction

Prayer Walking for Spiritual Breakthrough
The Complete Armor of God
The Weapons of Our Warfare
The Plan: satan's Agenda for Your Church